A Text Book Of

CELL BIOLOGY

T.Y.B.Sc. Zoology, ZY-336 : Paper VI, Semester III
As Per New Revised Syllabus with Effect from June 2015

Prin. Dr. Kishore R. Pawar
M.Sc., Ph.D.
Karmveer Abasaheb Alias,
N.M. Sonawane Arts, Science and Commerce
College, Satana. District - NASHIK.

Dr. Ashok E. Desai
M.Sc., Ph.D.
Associate Professor,
P.G. Department of Zoology, KTHM College,
NASHIK.

NIRALI
PRAKASHAN
ADVANCEMENT OF KNOWLEDGE

N1820

CELL BIOLOGY (T.Y.B.Sc. Zoology)   ISBN 978-93-5164-794-2

First Edition : June 2016

Published By :   Polyplate
NIRALI PRAKASHAN
Abhyudaya Pragati, 1312, Shivaji Nagar,
Off J.M. Road, Pune – 411005
Tel - (020) 25512336/37/39, Fax - (020) 25511379
Email : niralipune@pragationline.com

☞ **DISTRIBUTION CENTRES**

PUNE
Nirali Prakashan : 119, Budhwar Peth, Jogeshwari Mandir Lane, Pune 411002, Maharashtra
Tel : (020) 2445 2044, 66022708, Fax : (020) 2445 1538
Email : bookorder@pragationline.com, niralilocal@pragationline.com
Nirali Prakashan : S. No. 28/27, Dhyari, Near Pari Company, Pune 411041
Tel : (020) 24690204 Fax : (020) 24690316
Email : dhyari@pragationline.com, bookorder@pragationline.com
MUMBAI
Nirali Prakashan : 385, S.V.P. Road, Rasdhara Co-op. Hsg. Society Ltd.,
Girgaum, Mumbai 400004, Maharashtra
Tel : (022) 2385 6339 / 2386 9976, Fax : (022) 2386 9976
Email : niralimumbai@pragationline.com

☞ **DISTRIBUTION BRANCHES**

JALGAON
Nirali Prakashan : 34, V. V. Golani Market, Navi Peth, Jalgaon 425001,
Maharashtra, Tel : (0257) 222 0395, Mob : 94234 91860
KOLHAPUR
Nirali Prakashan : New Mahadvar Road, Kedar Plaza, 1st Floor Opp. IDBI Bank
Kolhapur 416 012, Maharashtra. Mob : 9850046155
NAGPUR
Pratibha Book Distributors : Above Maratha Mandir, Shop No. 3, First Floor,
Rani Jhanshi Square, Sitabuldi, Nagpur 440012, Maharashtra
Tel : (0712) 254 7129
DELHI
Nirali Prakashan : 4593/21, Basement, Aggarwal Lane 15, Ansari Road, Daryaganj
Near Times of India Building, New Delhi 110002
Mob : 08505972553
BENGALURU
Pragati Book House : House No. 1, Sanjeevappa Lane, Avenue Road Cross,
Opp. Rice Church, Bengaluru – 560002.
Tel : (080) 64513344, 64513355,Mob : 9880582331, 9845021552
Email:bharatsavla@yahoo.com
CHENNAI
Pragati Books : 9/1, Montieth Road, Behind Taas Mahal, Egmore,
Chennai 600008 Tamil Nadu, Tel : (044) 6518 3535,
Mob : 94440 01782 / 98450 21552 / 98805 82331,
Email : bharatsavla@yahoo.com

niralipune@pragationline.com | www.pragationline.com
Also find us on ⨍ www.facebook.com/niralibooks

PREFACE

We have great pleasure in presenting this book **'A Textbook of Cell Biology'** for the T. Y. B. Sc. Zoology students.

The present book is written as per the revised syllabus with effect from June 2015. The main objective of writing this book is to present the subject matter in a compiled, concise and easily comprehensive form keeping in mind the basic needs of the students.

This text book has been written in a simple and lucid language. Several illustrative figures and diagrams have been included in the text which will help the students to grasp the concepts quickly and easily. We strongly believe that this book will be of great help to students as well as teachers.

We are indebted to late Dr. V.N. Pawar, Sarchitnis, N.D.M.V.P. Samaj, Nashik for his inspiration and encouragement.

We are also thankful to Research Scholar Ms. Mrinmayee C. Datar and Research Fellow Ms. Sonali R. Deore for their timely suggestions.

We express our sincere thanks to Mr. Dineshbhai Furia and Jignesh Furia, Shri M. P. Munde and the staff of Nirali Prakashan for bringing out this book in time.

We would appreciate suggestions and feedback from colleagues and students for further improvement of the book.

June, 2016   **Prin. Dr. Kishore R. Pawar**
                                                              Dr. Ashok E. Desai

SYLLABUS

❖❖❖

CONTENTS

Chapter 1

INTRODUCTION TO CELL BIOLOGY

- CONTENTS -

1.1 INTRODUCTION

The cell is the smallest unit of the life. All living organisms are composed of single or many cells and cell products. The first compound microscope was described by **Robert Hooke** and he first observed and described the cells in 1665. He first used the term 'cell' to describe the hollow box-like cavities in cork. This was the beginning of new branch of biology the study of cell or cytology. After this discovery, many other scientists made the observations on the cell and its various components in the period of hundred years or so. Among them were the well known scientists **Lamark** (1809), **Detrochet** (1824) and **Turpin** (1826). The botanist Brown (1831), discovered that all plant cells possess nucleus. In 1838, Schleiden a German botanist studied plant cells and discovered that all tissues of plants are made up of cells. He emphasized that cells are organisms and all animals and plants are aggregation of these organisms arranged according to laws. The German Zoologist Schwann (1939) arrived at the same conclusion for animals. He stated that all the organisms are composed of essentially alike parts namely cells. This concept was then applied to all living organisms. The finding of **Schleiden and Schwann** that all living organisms consists of cells and cell products are now referred to as the cell theory or the cell principle.

According to the cell theory, all living organisms from the simplest unicellular organisms to very complex plants and animals, is composed of cells and cell products and each cell can act independently, but functions as an integral part of the complete organism. Though this cell theory is adopted by both Zoologists and Botanists but there were objections to this theory which explained most of the biological enzymes of those days. It was not free from errors. For example, Schwann believed that cells could be spontaneously generated by a process analogous to crystal formation. But studies of developing embryos showed that during growth, cells multiply themselves by cell division. These observations were summarized by **Kollikar** (1841) that sperms and ova are histological elements originating in the organisms. **Rudalf Virchow** (1855) expressed major expansion of the cell theory in his famous aphorism (proverb) that all cells arise from pre-existing cells. An animal arises only from an animal and the plant only from a plant. This established cell division as a central phenomena in the reproduction of organisms. Years later it was shown that cells ensure continuity between one generation and another by the mechanism of mitosis (**Flemming, 1880**) during which the precise partitioning of chromosomes occur (**Waldeyer, 1890**).

Another important discovery was that the development of an embryo starts with the fusion of two nuclei, one coming from an egg and the other from a sperm cell that was introduced into the egg during fertilization (**Hertwig, 1875**). Before the end of the 19th century, it was established that gametes (eggs and sperm cells) are formed by reduction of division, later called meiosis, by which number of chromosomes of a species remains constant from one generation to another.

All these discoveries led to the modern version of the cell theory, which states that :

(1) Cells are the morphological and physiological units of all living organisms.

(2) The properties of a given organism depend on those of its individual cells.

(3) Cells originate only from other cells and continuity is maintained through the genetic material.

(4) The smallest unit of life is the cell.

Thus, according to the cell theory, the cell is the smallest mass of protoplasm with nucleus, enveloped by permeable plasma membrane, which is capable of biosynthesis, energy transformation and self-reproduction.

However, certain primitive units of life such as *viruses* do not fulfil the fundamental requirements of the cell suggested by cell theory.

In the present state of knowledge the cell can be defined as simplest but complete expression of fundamental organisation and functions of all living organisms, covered by plasma membrane and capable of reproducing in a medium free of other living systems unlike the viruses.

1.2 PROKARYOTIC AND EUKARYOTIC CELLS

The body of all living organisms *(bacteria, blue green algae*, plants and animals) except viruses has cellular organisation and composed of single or many cells. The organisms which show only single cell in their body are called *unicellular organisms*. For example, bacteria, blue green algae, protozoa, etc. are unicellular. The organisms with many cells in their body are called *multicellular organism*. Most plants and animals are multicellular organisms. Thus, any cellular organism may contain either a

    (I) Prokaryotic cells or

    (II) Eukaryotic cells.

1.2.1 Prokaryotic Cells

The prokaryotic (Gr., *Pro* = primitive; *Karyon* = nucleus) cells are most primitive cells which occur in bacteria and blue green algae. These cells have primitive nuclei without nuclear envelope or membrane. The nuclear substances i.e. DNA, RNA, proteins etc. have direct contact with cytoplasm. The prokaryotic cells lack in cytoplasmic organelles like mitochondria, endoplasmic reticulum, golgi complex, lysosomes, centrioles, etc.

Bacteria

The bacteria are microscopic, single celled living organisms which do not possess chlorophyll. They are found in air, water and earth as well as in plants and animals. They show different shapes like rod-like **bacilli**, spherical *cocci* or *spiral spirilla* and *spirochetes* shapes. The various fatal diseases like diphtheria, typhoid, leprosy, tuberculosis etc. are caused by bacilli in man. The spherical forms or *gonococcus* causing gonorrhea in man. The spirochetes are spiral bacterial causing syphilis in man.

Ultra Structure of bacteria : The typical prokaryotic cell of bacteria contains an *outer covering and cytoplasm*. The outer covering is made of the following three layers :

(i) Plasma Membrane : The cytoplasm of the bacterial cells is enveloped by thin plasma membrane which is composed of lipid and protein molecules. It also contains oxidative or respiratory chain enzymes and multi enzymes complexes which perform the function of mitochondria in Eukaryotic cell. Plasma membrane also shows varied structures like sinks deep in cytoplasm forming *desmosomes (e.g. Thiovulvum majus)*. It may folded or showing invaginations in cytoplasm called *mesosomes (e.g. Bacillus subtilis)*. Mesosomes are useful as the respiratory organs and synthesize material for extracellular transport and for formation of cell wall.

(ii) Cell wall : The plasma membrane is enclosed by a strong, rigid *cell wall* and it contains carbohydrates, lipids, proteins phosphorous, organic salts, amino acids, muramic acid.

(iii) Capsule : The outer slimy layer of polysaccharides called capsule.

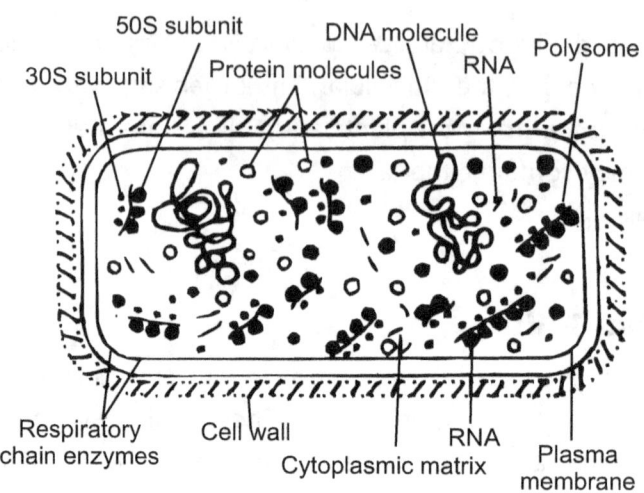

Fig. 1.1 : A prokaryotic cell of *Escherichia coli*

Cytoplasm

The cytoplasm of bacterial cell is dense, colloidal, with granules of glycogen, proteins and fats. Except ribosomes, mitochondria, lysomes, endoplasmic, reticulum and other organelle are absent. The ribosomes occur freely in cytoplasm and they form poly ribosomes during the process of protein synthesis. Certain photosynthetic bacteria show the presence of *chromatophores* having *bacteriochlorophyll*. In the central portion of the cytoplasm occur one or two nucleus like clear zones. Each zone contains a single, large, circular, doubled stranded DNA molecule which is called *bacterial chromosomes or genophores*. These distinct nuclear regions are called *nucleoids*. *Cocci* exhibit one nucleoid per cell, while rod like *bacilli* usually show one or more nucleoids per cell.

Flagella : Many bacteria are able to swim by beating of whip-like cellular outgrowth called *flagella*. The flagellum consists of a single fibril of 100 to 200 A°, thickness and several microns length originated from an intracellular *basal granule* through plasma membrane and cell wall. The fibril is largely made up of protein flagellin. Many bacteria show extracellular outgrowth on their cells which are hair-like processes called pilli or *fimbriae*. These are useful for the attachment of bacterial cell to solid substratum. They are composed of helically arranged *protein* called *pilin*.

Escherichia Coli

It is a non-pathogenic intestinal parasite of man and other mammals. It is gram-negative bacillus (i.e. unstainable by a strain developed by **C gram in 1885**). This organism is a very popular and favourite experimental organism for cell biologists. Advantage of this organism is that it proliferates rapidly and can be easily cultured in laboratory conditions.

E. coli is about 2 μm long and 0.8 to 1 μm thick and has outer cell wall of 100 A° thickness. Ultrastructurally, the cell of *E. coli* consists of an outer rigid cell wall plasma membrane and colloidal cytoplasm. The cytoplasm contains fat granules, different types of enzymes and different types of RNA (i.e. ribosomal RNA, messenger RNA, and transfer RNA). It also contains a large, double-stranded, circular DNA molecule of 1400 μ, length, diameter in each nucleoid is 0.2 μ. The DNA number may be one or two per cell. Cytoplasm also contains 20,000 to 30,000 ribosomes of 200 A° diameter which are main cellular organelles.

1.2.2 Eukaryotic Cells

The Eukaryotic cells (Gr. *eu* = good, *karyotic* = nucleated) possess true nucleus, i.e. the nuclear material such as DNA, RNA, nucleoplasm, all remain well separated from the cytoplasm by two porous lipoproteinous nuclear membranes. The eukaryotic cells are true cells, which occur in most plants (from algae to angiosperms) and animals (from protozoa to mammalia). These cells show different shapes and sizes.

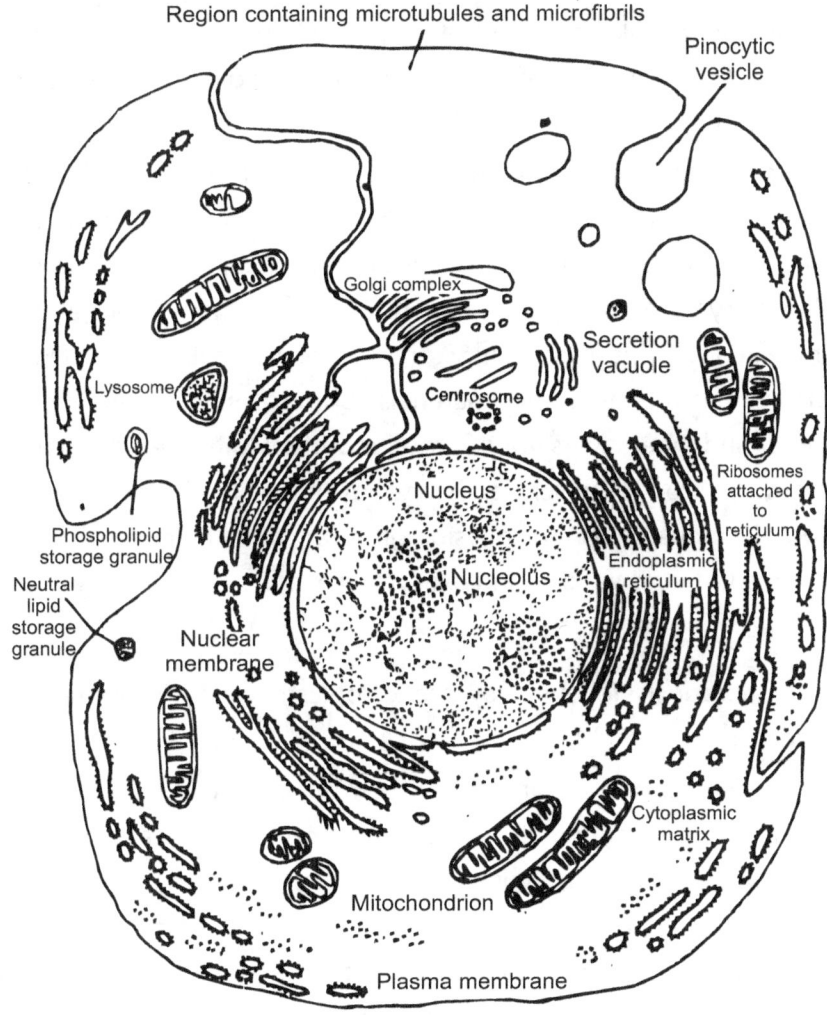

Fig. 1.2 : A typical Eukaryotic Animal Cell

The cells are larger than bacterial or prokaryotic cells. The size of the cells varies from 1μ to $175000\,\mu$ (175 mm). For example, ostrich egg is also a cell which is largest cell with 175 mm diameter. Nerve cells are the longest cells having length of 3 to 3.5 feet.

Ultra Structure

A typical eukaryotic cell consists of the following points :

1. Cell wall and plasma membrane.

2. Cytoplasm

3. Nucleus

1. Cell Wall and Plasma Membrane

In case of plant cell, the plasma membrane is usually protected by a thick rigid wall of cellulose called cell wall. It provides additional strength and ridigity to the plasma membrane of plant cells. The cell wall is absent in animal cells.

The plasma membrane is trilaminar membrane of lipid and protein molecules which forms the external covering. It is a living, ultra thin, elastic, porous, semipermeable membranous covering of cell. It primarily provides the mechanical support and external form to the protoplasm (cytoplasm + nucleus). The plasma membrane also delimits the protoplasm from exterior, checks the entry or exist of the substances. Due to its semi-permeable nature it transmits necessary materials to and from the cell. The ultra structure shows that the outer and inner layers are of proteins and middle layer is of lipids. The plasma membrane is porous through which exchange of molecules takes place. The plasma membrane performs various important physiological functions osmosis, diffusion or passive transport, active transport, endocytosis and exocytosis etc.

2. Cytoplasm

The plasma membrane is followed by the cytoplasm which is distinguished into the following structures :

(A) Cytoplasmic Matrix : The portion between membrane and nucleus is filled by an amorphous, translucent, homogenous liquid known as *cytoplamic* matrix or *hyaloplasm*. It is the complex mixture of various inorganic elements, salts and many organic molecules. The peripheral part is called *ectoplasm* and inner portion which is granular and less viscous is called *endoplasm*. The organic molecules are carbohydrates, lipids, proteins, nucleic acid (DNA, RNA), nucleo-proteins, nucleotides, amino acids, fatty acids and variety of enzymes.

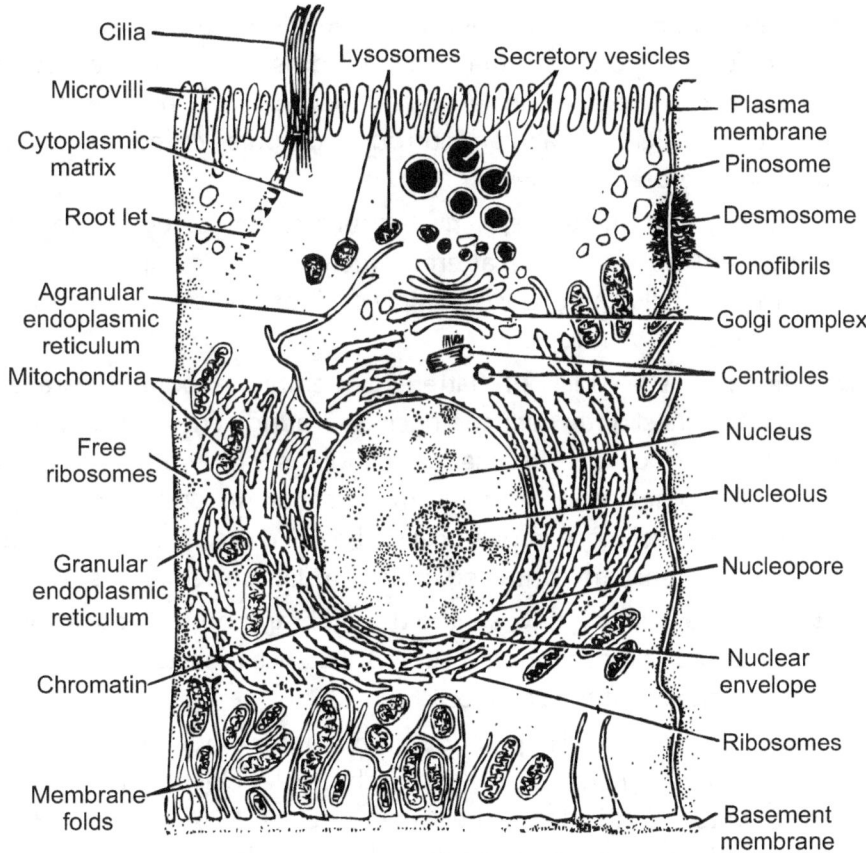

Fig. 1.3 : Structure of a Typical Eukaryotic Animal Cell

(B) Cytoplasmic Structures : There are certain living and non-living structures in cytoplasmic matrix. The non-living structures are *called paraplasm, deutoplasm* or *inclusions,* whereas the living structures are membrane bounded *organoides* or *organelles.* These both types of cytoplasmic structures can be studied under the following headings :

(i) Cytoplasmic inclusions : In the cytoplasmic matrix, many stored food granules and secretory substances of cell remain suspended in the form of refractile granules and form cytoplasmic inclusions. The cytoplasmic inclusions include oil drops, yolk granules, pigments, secretory granules and glycogen granules.

(ii) Cytoplasmic organoids or organelles : These are the living structures of the cytoplasm. The most important cytoplasmic organelles are endoplasmic reticulum, ribosomes, golgi complex, lysosomes, mitochondria, plastids, centrioles, cytoplasmic vacuoles micro tubules, basal granules, cilia and flagella. They perform various important biosynthetic and metabolic activities such as storage, synthesis, transportation, support and reproduction.

(1) **Endoplasmic reticulum :** The endoplasmic reticulum forms the network of inter connecting tubules and vesicles. After each cell division, it forms a nuclear envelope around the chromosomes (i.e. nucleus) and new plasma membrane between the dividing cells. It bears dense, granular and rounded bodies called ribosomes. They play an important role in protein synthesis.

(2) **Ribosomes :** They are minute spherical structures attached to the endoplasmic reticulum. They are also found scattered freely in the cytoplasm. Ribosomes are originated in the nucleolus and consist mainly of ribonucleic acid (r-RNA) and proteins. They are sites of protein synthesis.

(3) **Golgi complex :** It is a stack of flattened, membrane bound, parallely arranged organelle which occurs slightly near the nucleus around centrioles and has connection with endoplasmic recticulum. Its main function is storage of synthetic products (proteins) of ribosomes and endoplasmic reticulum and secretion of certain carbohydrates such as cellulose in plant cells. They also produce secretory granules e.g. acrosome, a digestive enzyme contained in the cap-like structure of sperms.

(4) **Lysosomes :** These are small, tiny, spheroid membrane bound vesicles which contain enzymes for intracellular digestion of foreign substances (bacteria etc.) and sometimes for the cellular organelles of the same cell.

(5) **Mitochondria :** They are rod shaped double membrane bound structures having the enzymes for respiratory metabolism. (e.g. Krebs cycle, electron transport chain, beta oxidation etc.) Mitochondria have their own circular DNA and ribosomes like the bacteria. They produce energy rich compound called adenosine triphosphate (ATP). So they are called *power house of the cell.*

(6) **Plastids :** These are mitochondria like structures of plant cells for the storage of the starch, pigments and other cellular products. The chlorophyll bearing plastid, the *chloroplast* has its own circular DNA molecule and capable of producing organic food by the process of photosynthesis.

(7) **Centrosomes :** They contain dense cytoplasm and are located near nuclei of animal cells. During cell division centrosome is found to contain two rod-shaped granules called *centrioles.* At the time of cell division the centrioles form the spindle structure of microtubules which help in the separation movement of chromosomes during last stages of cell division.

(8) **Cytoplasmic vacuoles :** These are small, liquid filled, structures useful for storage, transmission of materials and maintenance of internal pressure of the cell. They are found in plant and animal cells.

(9) **Microtubules :** The plant and animal cells contain many fine tubules called *microtubules* in the cytoplasm for transportation of water, ions, small molecules and formation of fibres or asters of the spindle during cell division.

(10) Basal granules : The animal or plant cells having locomotory organelles such as flagella or cilia contain spherical bodies called *basal granules* or *kinetosomes* at the base of flagella or cilia.

(11) Cilia and flagella : The cells of unicellular organisms and ciliated epithelium of multicellular organisms consists of hair-like cytoplasmic projections outside the surface of cell called cilia or flagella. They are useful for locomotion. Their structure shows nine outer fibrils around two large central fibrils.

3. Nucleus

It is usually a spheroid, centrally located cellular component which controls all the vital activities of the cytoplasm, regulate growth and reproduction of the cell and carries hereditary material, DNA in it. The nucleus consists of the following structures.

(i) Nuclear membrane or envelope : It is perforated envelope, occurs around the nucleus and made up of two lipoproteinous membranes. This membrane provides selective continuity between nuclear and cytoplasmic materials. It is continuous with the endoplasmic reticulum.

(ii) Nucleoplasm and chromatin fibres : The nucleus is filled with colloidal ground substance called *nucleoplasm*. It contains phosphoric acid, ribosomes and deoxyribose sugars, nucleotides and nucleic acid. The nucleoplasm contains thread-like elongated structures known as *chromosomes*. The chromosomes appear only during cell division. Otherwise, they occur in the form of ultra thin chromatin threads. They are also called *chromosomes* which consists of large molecules of DNA which remains wrapped in RNA and nucleoproteins.

(iii) Nucleolus : It is conspicuous, darkly stained, intranuclear spherical body which is accentric in position. Chemically, it contains large amount of ribosomal proteins and ribosomal RNA. It plays very important role in the process of protein synthesis and cell division. Its main function is biogenesis of ribosomes.

1.3 SHAPE OF CELLS

The eukaryotic cells or plant and animal cells exhibit various forms and shapes. The animal cells are generally spherical or oval but cell may be cubodial, polygonal, tubular, triangular, irregular or cylindrical in different plants and animals. The shape of the cell may vary from animal to animal and from organ to organ. Depending on the nature of function, the shape of the cell also shows variation. Even the cells of the same organ may display variations in shape.

In case of animal following different shapes are exhibited by the cells.

(1) Variable or constantly changing shape : The protozoan animal like *Amoeba* and *Leucocytes* display changing shape.

(2) Fixed shape : Majority of the cells show fixed shape which do not show the change.

    (i)   Cuboidal : It may be flattened, e.g. squamous epithelium, endothelium and the upper layer of epidermis.

    (ii) Cuboidal : The cells of thyroid gland follicles are cuboidal in shape.

    (iii) Columnar : The cells lining the intestine are columnar in shape.

    (iv) Discoidal : The erythrocytes or red blood cells of vertebrates are disc-like.

    (v)   Spherical : The eggs of many animals are rounded or spherical in shape.

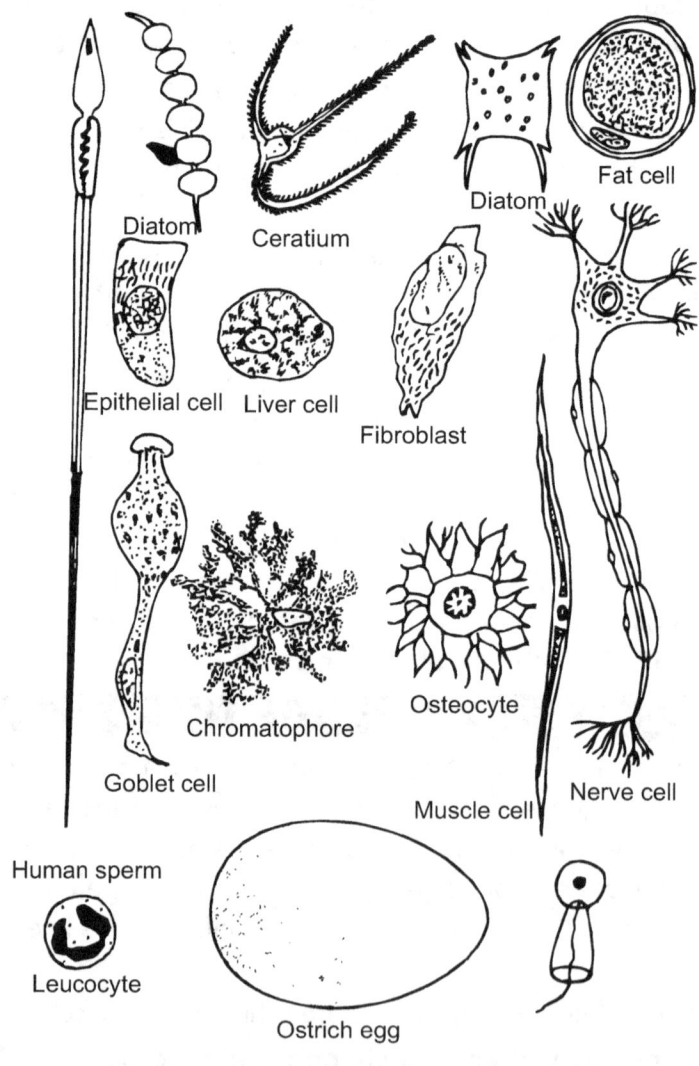

Fig. 1.4 : Various Types of Eukaryotic Cells Showing Different Shapes

(vi)   Spindle shaped : The smooth muscle cells are elongated and spindle shaped.

(vii) Elongated : Nerve cells are elongated in shape.

(viii) Branched : The pigment or chromatophore cells of skin are branched.

1.4 SIZE OF THE CELLS

The size of the cells vary from very small cells of bacteria (0.2 to 5.0 μ) to a very large egg of the Ostrich (175 mm in diameter). The Ostrich egg is considered as largest cell. The longest nerve cells have been found to have the length of 92 to 1.06 metre. The following factors governing the size of the cell.

(i)   The nucleocytoplasmic ratio : It is the ratio between the volume of the nucleus and the cytoplasm.

(ii) The ratio of the cell surface to the cell volume.

(iii) The rate of metabolism.

Points to Remember

- The prokaryotes are the most primitive organisms.
- Prokaryotic organisms do not have a true nucleus.
- Eukaryotic cells possess a membrane-bound nucleus.
- Bacteria are microscopic, single celled, living organisms which do not possess chlorophyll.
- The bacterial cell wall is made up of peptidoglycan.
- The cell wall prevents osmotic lysis of cell and gives shape and rigidity to the bacterial cell.

Exercise

1. Describe the ultra structure of a prokaryotic cell.
2. Describe the structure of a typical bacterial cell.
3. Draw a labelled diagram of prokaryotic cell.
4. Draw a labelled diagram of eukaryotic cell.
5. Give an account of the structure of an animal cell and state the functions which are attributed to its component parts.
6. Draw a labelled diagram of an animal cell.
7. Give the distinguishing features of prokaryotic and eukaryotic cell.
8. Differentiate between plant and animal cells.
9. What is cell? Give an account of different shapes and sizes of cells.
10. Describe the structure and functions of animal cell.

11. Write short notes on
    a. Prokaryotic cell
    b. Eukaryotic cell
    c. Nucleus
    d. Shape and size of cells.
12. Define / Explain.
    a. Prokaryotic cell
    b. Eukaryotic cell
    c. Cell

PLASMA MEMBRANE

- CONTENTS -

All the cells are covered by a very thin membrane called *Plasmalemma* which is not visible under the light microscope. Under light microscope the structure seen is called cell membrane. This cell membrane is made up of plasmalemma and surrounding cell cement. The plasma membrane may be protected by other coverings e.g. plasma membrane of the egg is surrounded by the vitelline membrane and the jelly layer, both of which are secreted by the ovary.

2.1 CHEMICAL COMPOSITION

Plasma membrane is made up of lipoproteins. These are special non-bonded combinations of lipids with proteins. Generally, membranes contain about 60% protein and 40% carbohydrates by dry weight.

2.1.1 Proteins

Plasma membrane contains three different types of proteins namely, *structural proteins, enzymes* and *carrier proteins.* The structural proteins form the back bone of the cell membrane and the average molecular weight of structural proteins is 3×10^4. Enzymes are also a major component of the plasma membrane and they are catalytic protiens. Carrier proteins are also called permeases and they transport substances across the membrane against concentration gradient. Their molecular weight is similar to that of structural proteins.

The proteins of plasma membrane are of two types : namely intrinsic or integral proteins and extrinsic or peripheral proteins.

Plasma Membrane Proteins

(1) **Spectrin :** It is the most abundant protein which is long fibrous molecule that constitutes about 30% of the membrane protein mass. It is useful for maintaining the biconcave shape of the RBCs.

(2) **Ankyrin :** Spectrin interacts indirectly via this protein.

(3) **Glycophorin :** It is present on the outer surface of the red blood cell. Its function is unknown.

(4) **Enzymes :** More than 30 enzymes have been detected in isolated plasma membranes. Those most constantly found are 5'-nucleotidase, Mg^{2+}ATPse, Na^+ -K^+ ATPase, alkaline phosphatase, adenyl cyclase, RNAse. These enzymes are important in ion transfer across the plasma membrane.

(5) **Glycoproteins :** In erythrocytes membranes, hexose and hexosamine fucose are bound to proteins. They are present on the outer surface of the membrane. These proteins are attached to oligosaccharides, thus forming glycoproteins.

(6) **Intergral (Intrinsic) and Peripheral (Extrinsic) proteins :** Spectrin and glycoproteins are examples of these proteins.

2.1.2 Lipids

There are two types of lipids associated with plasma membrane. They are called polar lipids. These lipids contain hydrophilic heads and hydrophobic tails and these two regions are connected by glycerol moiety, a splingosine derivative or a sterol.

In the plasma membrane, phospholipids, glycolipids and sterols are present.

Plasma Membrane Lipid

(1) Phospholipids : Most abundant

(2) Cholesterol : A hydrophobic four-membered fused ring structure.

(3) Glycolipids : Oligosaccharide containing lipid molecule.

They have water loving or hydrophilic or polar end and a hydrophobic or water hating or non-polar end. They influence fluidity of the membrane.

Plasma membrane Carbohydrates : Carbohydrates are present in the plasma membrane in the form of glycolipids and glycoproteins on the external membrane surface. The oligosaccharide chains play an important role in cell to cell recognition processes.

2.2 MEMBRANE MODELS

For the study of physical and biological features of plasma membrane two types of models have been proposed. These are *bilayer models and unicellular or subunit models.*

In bilayer models, it is belived that proteins and lipids occur in layers. Whereas in the unicellular models membrane is believed to consist of a number of similar units.

2.2.1 Bilayer Model

Bilayer model consists of the following three types :

1. Lipid membrane.
2. Protein lipid protein.
3. Models in which proteins are considered to penetrate the lipid layer.

1. Lipid membrane : Overton (1895) found that fat soluble substances passes easily through the cell membrane. He concluded by this observation that cell membrane contained lipids, plasma membrane shows presence of lipid layer was confirmed by experiments on wetting cell surface with oil. When oil drop comes in contact with cell it spreads over and adheres to the cell surface.

The possible structure of plasma membrane was first proposed by Gorter and Grendel (1925) in erythrocytes. They found that the surface membrane was composed of a double layer of lipid molecules.

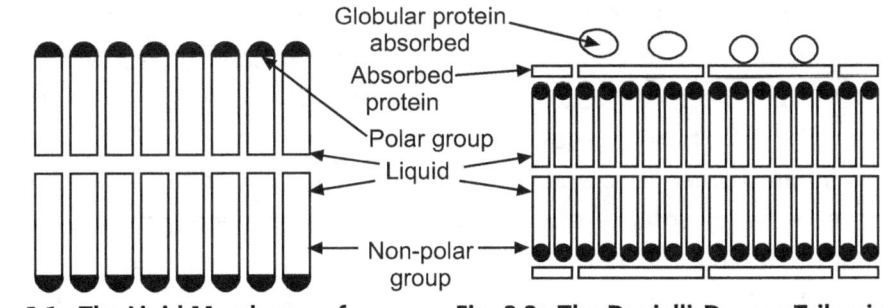

Fig. 2.1 : The Lipid Membrane of   Fig. 2.2 : The Danielli-Davson Trilaminar
Gorter and Grendel (1925)   Sandwich Model of the Cell Membrane

2. Protein lipid protein (sandwich models) : Davson and Danielli (1935) proposed the lipoprotein model of the cell membrane. In this model, the two lipid layers with polar regions are on the outer side. The globular proteins are associated with the polar groups of lipid.

The Unit Membrane : Robertson (1935) proposed his unit membrane model for plant and animal cells. According to this model, all the cell organelles also possess unit membrane structure indicating its cellular universality. Under electron microscope, it shows dense layers separated by a clear zone. The unit membrane is considered to be trilaminar with two outer protein layers separated by bimolecular lipid layer. The unit membrane is 75 A° thick, with a 35 A° lipid layer between the two. Thus, it resembles the Danielli-Davosn model.

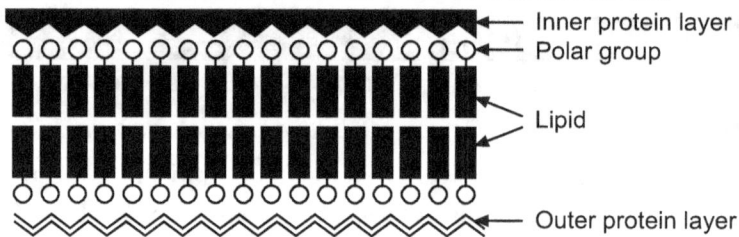

Fig. 2.3 (a) : The Unit Membrane Structure

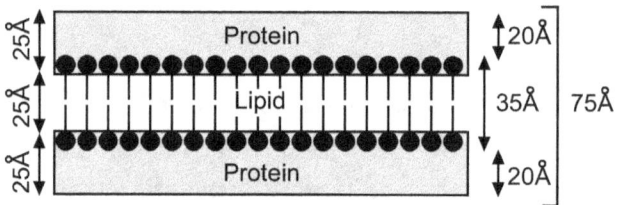

Fig. 2.3 (b) : The Unit Membrane (Modified from Robertson, 1959)

3. Models in which proteins are considered to penetrate the lipid layers : According to some cell biologists there are no proteins on the outside of lipid layer as in the *Danielli-Davson model*; but are considered to partially or fully penetrate the lipid layer. This model explains low surface tension of biological membranes like protein-lipid-protein model.

2.2.2 Fluid-Mosaic Model

The fluid-mosaic model of plasma membrane was proposed by *Singer* and *Nicolson* in 1972 and it was widely accepted as compared to other proposed models. The important feature of this model is that the biological membranes are considered to be quasifluid (half fluid) structures in which the lipids and integral proteins are arranged in a mosaic manner. The reason for the wide acceptance of the model is that, it very well explains the properties of cell membrane. The model assumes that there is a peripheral layer of *phospholipid* molecules in which peripheral and integral *globular proteins* are embedded to varying degrees. Thus, the proteins are compared to ice bergs floating on a sea of the phospholipid bilayer. During certain immunological experiments, the attachment of antibodies to cell surface exposed integral membrane proteins such as glycophorin which led to the realisation that membrane proteins are not fixed within the lipid bilayer but are free to move laterally, like ice berges floating submerged in a sea of lipid (Fig. 2.5). This observation inspired the name *fluid mosaic model,* coined by Singer and Nicolson. This model considers that lipid-protein association to be *hydrophobic* but the *Danielli-Davson* model assumes *hydrophilic* bonding between lipids and proteins. The fluidity of the membrane is the result of this hydrophobic interaction. The phospholipids and many intrinsic proteins are *amphipatic* molecules, i.e. both hydrophilic and hydrophobic groups occur within the same molecule.

The globular proteins which occur in the membrane are of two types, namely, *extrinsic* or *peripheral* proteins and *intrinsic* or *integral* proteins. The peripheral proteins are soluble and readily dissociate from the membrane. They are present entirely outside the lipid bilayer. While the integral proteins are relatively insoluble and dissociate with difficulty. Some proteins may partially penetrate through the surface of the lipid bilayer. While others may penetrate directly through the lipid bilayer.

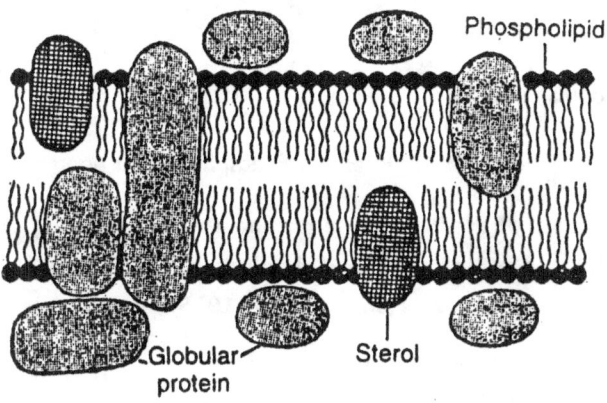

Fig. 2.4 (a) : Schematic Representation of a Section Through a Eukaryotic Fluid-mosaic Membrane

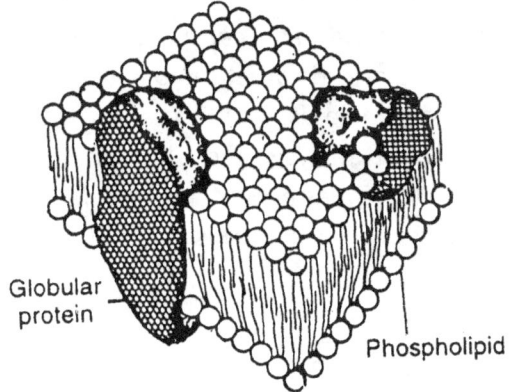

Fig. 2.4 (b) : The fluid-mosaic Model of Singer and Nicolson (1972) : Bacteria Membrane

Such proteins are in contact with the aqueous solvent on both sides of the membrane. The integral proteins are amphipatic having both hydrophilic and hydrophobic groups. Their hydrophobic polar heads protrude from the surface of the membrane, while non-polar regions are embedded in the interior of the membrane. The integral proteins are capable of lateral diffusion in the lipid bilayer.

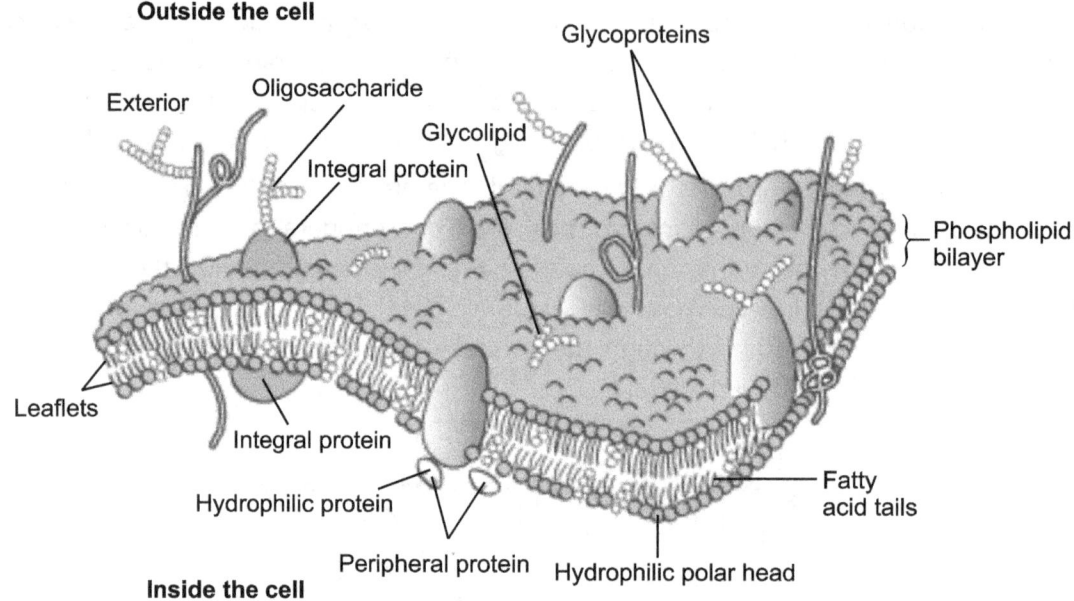

Fig. 2.5 : Fluid-mosaic Model of the Plasma Membrane. Proteins floating on a sea of lipid. Some Proteins Span the Lipid Bilayer, others are exposed only to one surface or the other (Modified after De. Robertis et al.; 1975)

2.2.3 Lipid Bilayer

When phospholipids are dispersed in water they form a lipid bilayer. The polar heads of the lipid molecules project into aqueous phase. The hydrophobic chains aggregate together.

The mosaic nature of the membrane has been proved by the results of freeze-etching techniques in which protein particles are shown at the plane of cleavage of the bilayer (Tillack and Marchesi, 1970). The fluidity of the lipids is supported by many indirect studies based on X-ray diffraction, differential thermal analysis and electron spin techniques (Hubbell and McConnell, 1971). The fluidity of the integral proteins is supported by experiments on cell fusion (Frye and Edidin, 1970) and on those of clustering and 'capping' of surface antigens (Edidin and Frambrough, 1973).

Thus, the lipid bilayer shows the following dynamic motional properties such as :

(i) Flexon : Rapid internal motion involving flexing within each lipid molecule.

(ii) Rapid lateral diffusion of lipids.

(iii) **Flip-flop motion** in which transfer of lipid molecules from one side of bilayer to the other.

(iv) **Rotation :** The lipid molecules might rotate about their axes.

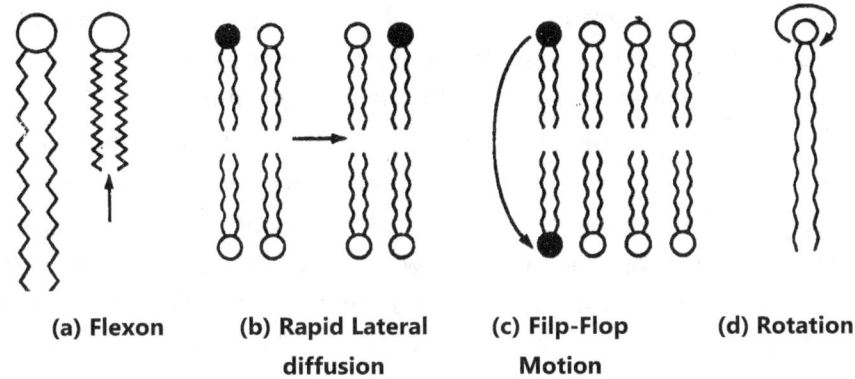

(a) Flexon	**(b) Rapid Lateral**	**(c) Filp-Flop**	**(d) Rotation**
	diffusion	**Motion**	

Fig. 2.6 : Motional Properties of the Lipid Bilayer

Because of rapid movements of lipid and protein molecules, the membrane is considered to be highly fluid. The proteins of the membrane are concerned with enzymatic activity of membrane, functions as receptors to external stimuli transport of molecules and a receptor function. The lipid bilayer provides the permeability barrier.

2.2.4 Functions of Cell Membrane

(1) Transport : The membrane which allows the passage of a solvent but not of a solute is called as a semipermeable membrane. A membrane which permits one substance to pass through more easily than another is said to be selectively permeable because it allows the passage of both solvent are solute. Molecules diffuse from a region of greater concentration to a region of lower concentration. The difference in the levels of the two concentrations is called the concentration gradient. Osmosis is the diffusion of water (or a solvent) across a membrane in response to the concentration gradient. Transport of molecules across the membrane may be active or passive. In active transport, molecules usually move from regions of low concentration to regions of high concentration i.e. against concentration gradient. Thus, it requires energy and depends upon ATP supply. In passive transport, the passage of molecules through membrane from a high concentration region to a low concentration region. Transport of metabolites across the membrane along the concentration gradient and without the use of a carrier molecule is called simple diffusion.

(2) Cell recognition and adhesion : The mammalian leucocytes recognize foreign cells like bacteria and engulf them by phagocytosis. The sites for cell recognition are known to lie on the surface of the plasma membrane.

(3) Antigen specificity : The glycoproteins on the surface of the cell membrane determine the antigen specificities of the cell. The different blood group systems are all based on the antigenic properties of erythrocytic cell membranes. The ABO blood group system is based on the relationships between antigens on R.B.C. and antibodies in blood serum. The antigenic determinants on the surface of erythrocytes are mainly glycolipids.

(4) Hormone transport : Hormores control the metabolism of cells. The cell membrane contains receptors which recognize specific hormones and convey the information to the interior of the cell. This stimulates a change in the metabolism of the cell.

(5) Oxidative phosphorylation : The inner membrane of the mitochondria and the plasma membrane of bacteria contain the electron transport chain which plays an important part in cell respiration. This chain consists of a series of components which can transfer electrons. Electrons from substrates pass down the chain resulting in reduction and oxidation of each component. During this process there is a decrease in free energy, about half of which is utilized for the synthesis of ATP. This process is called oxidative phosphorylation.

(6) Endocytosis and exocytosis : In certain cell endocytosis is an important activity in which material is transported into cells by formation of vesicles. It includes two processes namely *phagocytosis* (cell eating) and *pinocytosis* (cell drinking). Exocytosis is process in which membrane lined material is removed from the cell.

(7) Chemoreception : Molecules associated with the cell membrane respond to a variety of stimuli. Chemoreception or the response to chemical stimuli is shown by a variety of organisms from bacterial to mammals.

(8) Transmission : The transmission of nerve impulses takes place at the membrane surface of nerve cells.

2.3 MEMBRANE RECEPTORS

Membrane receptors are macro-molecules that have the dual function of recognizing a chemical signal and initiating a biological response. Several cellular regulatory agents (e.g. peptide hormones neutro-transmitters) are called ligands. They act as chemical signals, which are recognised by such receptors. At the receptor site there is a specific type of binding that involves a ligand receptor interaction. Several kinds of receptors produce a response by interacting with the enzyme adenylate cyclase within the membrane which produces cyclic AMP from ATP. Several receptors that are specific for different ligands may act on a single type of adenylate cyclase. The important point is that the effect of the ligands is not additive, in other words, the system behaves as though several receptors are coupled to one molecule of enzyme. To explain this phenomenon *Cuatrecasas* and others have postulated *mobile hypothesis* which is based on fluidity of the membrane.

According to this hypothesis the lateral diffusion of receptors and enzyme within the plane of the lipid bilayer allows several receptors to couple with a single adenylate cyclase.

This hypothesis is confirmed experimentally by fusion studies. Cells having the β–adrenergic receptor in their membrane were fused with others containing only adenylate cyclase. The resulting hybrid cells contained both macromolecules, enabling coupling between the receptor and adenylate cyclase to occur. In these hybrid cells, under the influence of the ligand (in case of isoproterenol) there was production of cAMP, the original hybridized cells were unresponsive to the ligand.

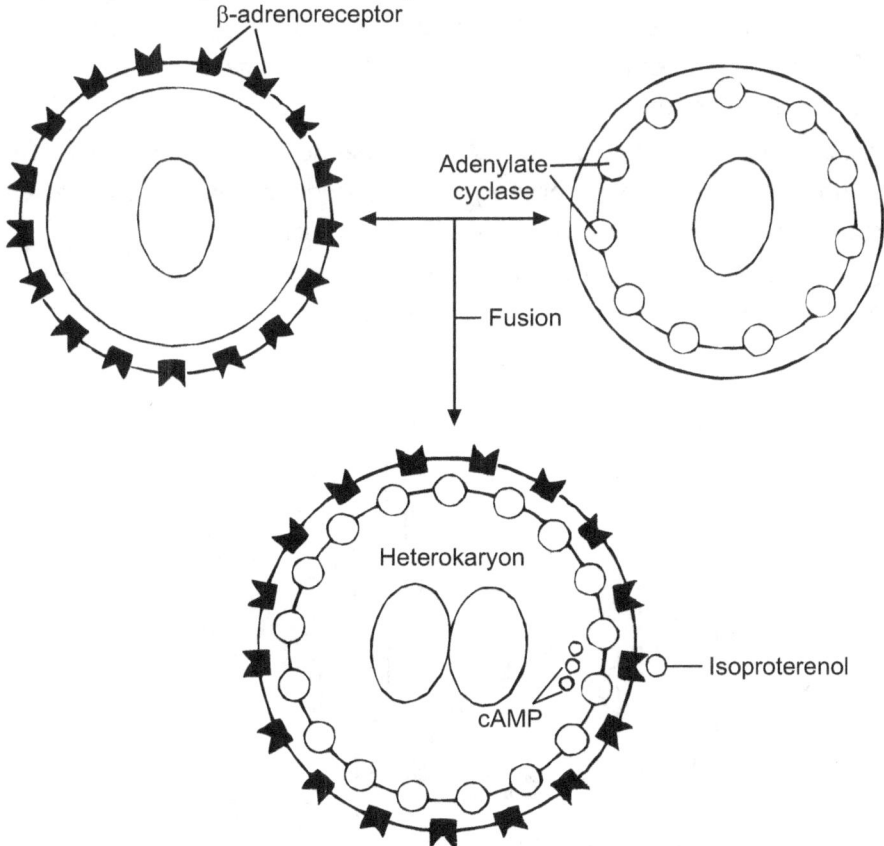

Fig. 2.7 : Cell containing the β-adrenergic Receptor Fused with Another Carrying only Adenylate Cyclase. The Heterokaryon contains both Components and can now Couple under the Action of the Specific Ligand Isoproterenol Resulting in the Production of cAMP.

2.4 MODIFICATIONS OF PLASMA MEMBRANE

2.4.1 Microvilli

The plasma membrane shows number of specializations or modifications on cell surfaces. The narrow invaginations or finger like projections of plasma membrane at the cell surface are known as *microvilli*. The columnar epithelial cells of intestine have to perform active absorption of digested food. The microvilli lack the internal filaments or tubules found in cilia. The microvilli of intestine are 0.6 to 0.8 μm long and only 0.1 μm in diameter. These are devices for increasing effective surface area for absorption. A single cell may contain as many as 3000 microvilli. In case of intestinal, epithelial cells, a dense mat of delicate branching tangled filaments cover (fuzzy coat) the surface of microvilli which appear to resist attack from digestive enzymes. It is composed of glycoprotein macro-molecules.

The core of microvilli is traversed by longitudinal microfilaments. These filaments contain actin (a protein) are attached at the tip of microvilli by a α-actin. They are useful for contraction of microvilli. There are other filaments of protein called *fimbrin* and *villin*. These bind and cross link the F-action.

At the bases, they are joined together by transverse network of microfilaments extending between the junctional complexes forming terminal web or bar. Interminal web, besides actin, also present myosin, α-actinin, tropomyosin and spectrin.

In the poison gland of scorpion modified microvilli are found, where the microvilli soon after origin, branch into large number of secondary branches called dendric microvilli.

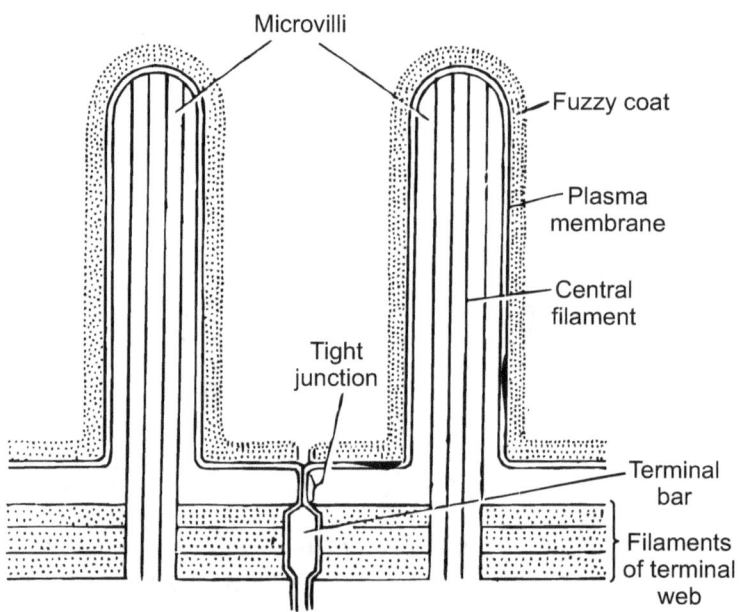

Fig. 2.8 : Microvilli

(1) Caveolae : These are cave like invaginations of the cell surface, first named by Yamada in (1955) which form blind tubular pouches, opening to the extracellular spaces. These may be small as found in vertebrate capillary endothelial cell, but more definite functional attributes can be assigned to many caveolae. They may act as transient membrane association with secretion and with uptake of materials into the cell by endocytosis. Many small caveolae and vesicles may be secretary in nature.

(2) Functional Complexes : Sometimes characteristics junctional complexes have been shown operating for keeping the adjacent cells together. Electron microscopic studies have shown that these junctional complexes are broadly identified as :

(a) Tight junctions (Zona Occludens)

(b) Gap junctions (Nexus)

Desmosomes which are :

(i) Belt desmosomes or intermediary junctions (zona adherens)

(ii) Spot desmosomes comprising of *Macula adherens*

(iii) Hemidesmosomes

(iv) Septate desmosomes.

(1) Tight Junctions (Zona Occludens) : It is located at the distal region between the adjacent cells where actual fusion of the outer membrane of the adjoining cells occurs. As a result, a single intermediate layer is formed and produce an apparent five layered unit at that region. It acts as seal with no intracellular space. Tight junctions are abundant in the collector tube of kidney. It appears as a network of ridges on the cytoplasmic half of the membrane, with complimentary grooves in the outer half. The ridges appear to be composed of two rows of particles, each one belonging to the adjacent cells.

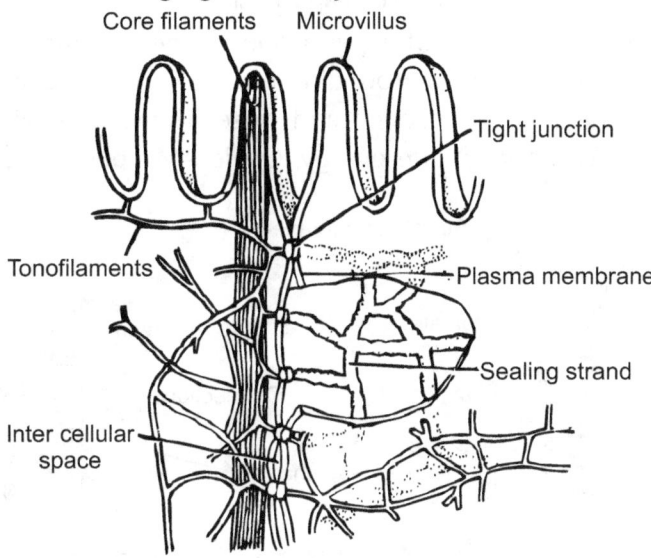

Fig. 2.9 : Tight Junction

The lines of these particles produce the sealing and therefore have been named sealing stands. Tight junctions are barrier to the diffusion of macro-molecules or lipid in the bilayer.

(2) Gap Junctions (Nexus of Fascia Occludens) : These are called as communicating junctions located at specialized region of contact between opposed plasma membranes of the adjacent cells. It permits direct transfer of ions and other small molecules between cells without traversing the extra cellular space. The gap junction is characterized by a 2-4 nm (20 A°) space between two membranes. The gap is filled with densely packed protein particles each of which appears to be a channel that connects the two cells. In tangential section, gap junctions show hexagonal array of 8-9 nm particles. At the centre of each particle there is channel. They represent regions in which there are junctional channels (1.5 to 2 nm in diameter) through which ions and small molecules can pass from one cell to other. Cells having gap junctions are electrically coupled i.e. there is a free flow of electric current carried by ions.

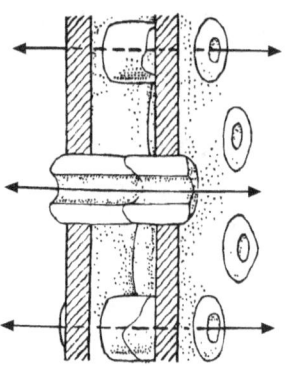

Fig. 2.10 : Gap Junction

The macromolecular unit structure of gap junction has been named the 'connexon' which appears as an annulus of 6-sub-units surrounding the channel. It is believed that the sliding of the subunits causes the channel to open and close. The permeability of the channel is regulated by Ca^{++} and ATP provides the energy. Cyclic AMP plays a regulatory role in the formation of gap junction.

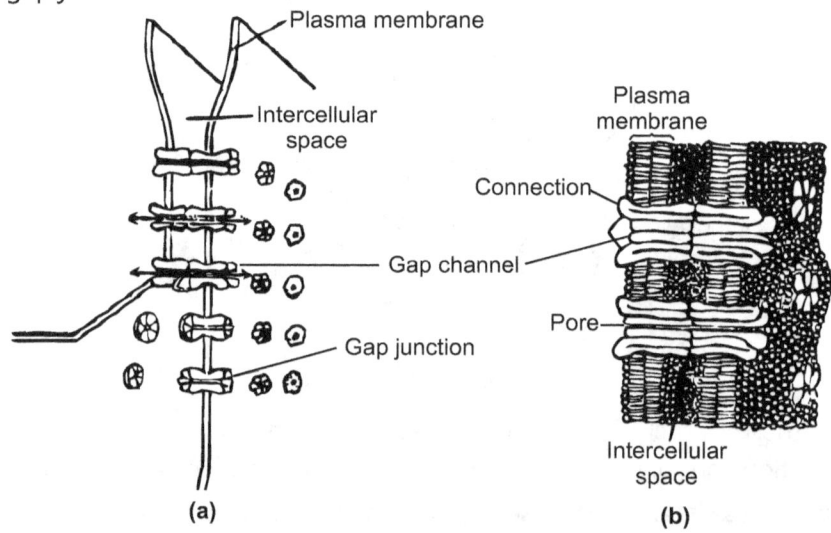

Fig. 2.11 : (a) Gap Junction Between Two Cell

(b) Finner Structure of the Connexon or Junctional Unit.

2.4.2 Desmosomes

Desmosomes are button like points of strong adhesion between adjacent cells in a body tissue. This cell-cell adhesion gives the tissue structural integrity, enabling the cells to function as a unit and to resist stress. Desmosomes are found in many tissues but they are especially abundant in cells of skin, heart muscle, and the neck of the uterus. Desmosomes form early in embryonic development and play an important role in maintaining cell position during development.

The plasma membranes of the two adjacent cells are aligned in parallel, separated by a space of about 25-35 nm. The extracellular space between the two membranes is called the desmosome core. A thick plaque is found just beneath the plasma membrane of each of the two adjoining cells. The desmosome core is filled with filaments and granules of proteins called desmocollins and desmogleins. These are cadherins that interact with the plaque at the inner membrane surface and mediate cell-cell adhesion at the outer membrane surface.

Cadherins

The second category of cell-surface glycoproteins are collectively called Cadherins. Cadherins are of three subtypes such as :

(i) E-cadherin,

(ii) N-cadherin and

(iii) P-cadherin.

The first category of cell surface glycoprotein is known as Neural Cell Adhesion Molecule or N-CAM which operates in the early embryonic development and is found on the surface of nerve cells and glial cells and causes them to stick together by C^{++} independent mechanism.

E-cadherin is found on many types of epithelial cells, N-cadherin on nerve, heart and lens cells and P-cadherin on cells in the placenta and epidermis. These three cadherins are homologous transmembrane glycoprotein and are made of 700 aminoacid residues. They play important roles in later stages of vertebrate development because their appearance and disappearance correlate with major morphogenetic events in which tissue segregate from one another.

Unlike E-cadherin, desmocollins and desmogleins probably interact heterophilically across the intercellular space. Like other cadherins, linker proteins bind to their cytosolic tail and link them to the cytoskeleton. The β-catenin family protein *plakoglobin* binds to the desmocollin, plakoglobin in turn binds to a plakin protein called *desmoplakin*. Desmoplakin in turn attaches to *tonofilaments* which are composed of intermediate filaments such as *vimentin, desmin* or *keratin*.

Tonofilaments extend inward from the plaque, anchoring the desmosome in the cytoplasm. The main protein present in the tonofilaments is the intermediate filament keratin, desmin, or vimentin, depending on the cell type. Each desmosome has anchoring sites for intermediate filaments in the cells on both sides of the junction, thereby linking the intermediate filaments of adjacent cells and forming continuous cytoskeletal network throughout the tissues.

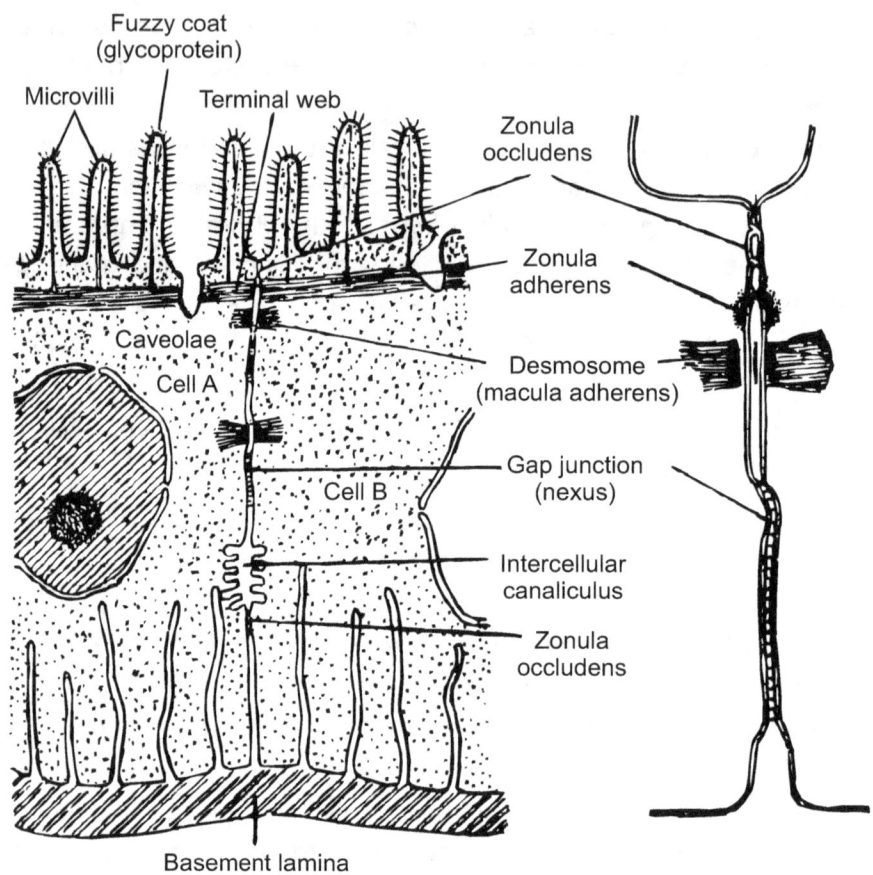

Fig. 2.12 : Desmosome

Tonofilaments

Tonofilaments are also called keratin filaments. These are complex class of intermediate filaments which consists of prekeratin or cytokeratin filaments. These filaments anchor to the cell surface and tend to converge upon the desmosomes.

In man, there are as many as 19 different cytokeratins. Tonofilaments are not contractile. They form a structural framework for the cell cytoplasm. Mammalian cytokeratins are α-fibrous proteins that are synthesized in cells of the living layers of epidermis. They are composed of multiple polypeptides ranging in size between 47,000 to 58,000 daltons and have a three chain structural unit.

Cytoskeleton

The network of fibres found in the cell are known as cytoskeleton. The fibre of the cytoskeleton extend throughout the cell having inter connection with cell membrane and cell organelles. It represents some fibrous proteins of the cytoplasm which help to maintain cell shape and to give contractibility to the cell. It also helps to facilitate communication among intracellular organelles. It also helps in cell locomotion or the movement of protoplasm, i.e. cyclosis.

Cytoskeleton consists of three components, the thickest tubular component called *microtubules*, thinnest fibres called *microfilaments* and fibres of intermediate thickness called *intermediate filaments*.

Types of Desmosomes

There are three main types of desmosomes, namely belt desmosomes, spot desmosomes and hemidesmosomes.

(1) Belt Desmosomes (Zonula Adherans) : These are formed at the interface between columnar cells just below the free surface. It is also called terminal bar or intermediary junction.

Under electron microscope the belt desmosomes form a band that girdles the inner surface of the cell membrane. This band possess a web of 6 nm actin microfilaments and another group of interwoven intermediate filaments or tonofilaments of 10 nm. Actin filaments are contractile whereas intermediate filaments play a structural role.

(2) Spot Desmosomes (Macula Adherans) : It is also called a fastening body or a binding body. These are disc or circular points of contact about 0.5 μm is diameter between the plasma membranes of adjacent cells. They are separated by a distance of 30-50 nm.

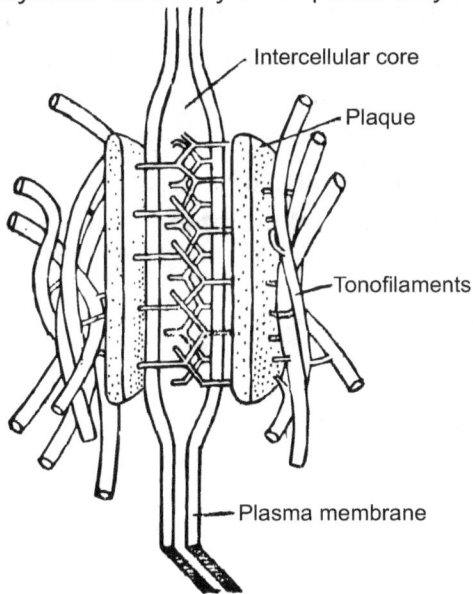

Intercellular core

Plaque

Tonofilaments

Plasma membrane

Fig. 2.13 : Spot Desmosome

The spot desmosomes consists of a disc shaped plaque (0.5 µm diameter) on the cytoplasmic surface of each cell membrane. Non-contractile tonofilaments form the structural framework of cytoplasm are attached to the plaques. Thin filaments called trans membrane linkers or desmocollins arising from the plaques fill the intercellular gap between the membranes.

They provide mechanical coupling. Sometimes a discontinuous middle dense line of coating material may be observed in the intracellular core. Cellular adhesion at the desmosomes depends mainly on this extracellular coating material.

(3) Hemidesmosomes : In the basal region of some epithelial cells, only half desmosomes may be present, called hemidesmosomes.

They are useful as a anchoring sites for bundles of tonofilaments and also for joining the cell membrane of epithelial cells to the underlying basement membrane.

(4) Septate Desmosomes : Wood (1959), Lock and Gauranten (1967) have reported different types of desmosomes in the epithelia of invertebrates and named them as septate desmosomes. In these desmosomes, the two plasma membrane remain separated by a distance of 150 A° -200 A° and both remain joined by many transverse parallel septa. These septa are found to be continuous upto outer proteinous layers of plasma membranes. These desmosomes lack the intracellular cementing substance and tonofilaments of the desmosomes. They act like attachment or adhesive devices of cells and they also permit intercellular communication and electrical coupling

(5) Terminal Bars (Zonula adherans) : The terminal bars are also known as intermediary junctions or zonula adherans. The terminal bars are similar to desmosomes except that they lack the tonofibrils. In terminal bars, the plasma membrane is thickened and the cytoplasm of thickened area is dense. The terminal bars occur in the intermediate portion of the plasma membrane of columnar cells just below the surface.

(6) Inter-digitations : At some places the plasma membrane of two adjacent cells gives out finger like projections known as inter-digitations. The inter-digitations may become further complicated by the development of desmosomes and terminal bars etc.

Classification of Desmosomes

Desmosomes are classified in several ways :

(A) According to shape :

(i) **Macular Desmosomes :** They are have spot like shape and often called maculae adherans.

(ii) **Zonula Desmosomes :** Those which encircle a cell like a belt or zone and bind it to its neighbours all around its circumference at the level of the Zonular desmosome often called terminal bars.

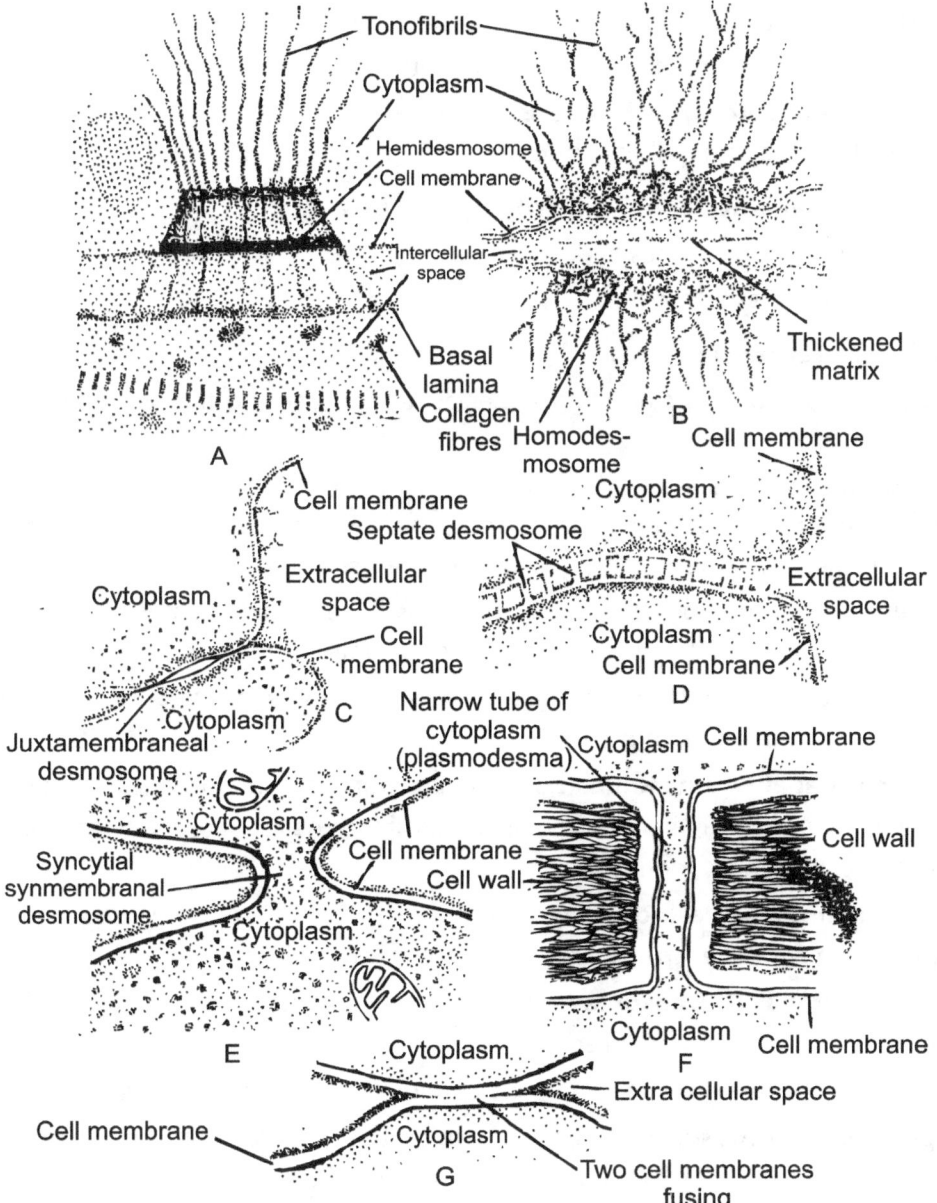

Fig. 2.14 : Different types of Desmosomes

(B) According to the structure to which cell surface is bound at desmosome :

(i) Antodesmosomes : Those which bind an areas of cell surface to another desmosome on another area of the surface of the same cell.

(ii) Homodesmosomes : Those bind an area of cell surface of one cell to a desmosome on the cell surface of another cell. They may be either :

Isodesmosomes : Binding one cell to another of the same type or

Allodesmosomes : Binding one cell to another cell of a different type.

(iii) **Heterodesmosomes or Hemidesmosomes :** Those which bind an area of cell surface to some non-cellular structure.

(C) According to similarity or dissimilarity of structure :

(i) Symmetrical Desmosomes

(ii) Asymmetrical Desmosomes.

(D) According to function :

(i) **Adherent Desmosomes :** Highly specialized for resisting tensile forces. They are all filamentous.

(ii) **Occluding Desmosomes :** Useful for sealing one cell membrane to the other and form barrier to diffusion and fluid exchanges between one extracellular fluid compartment and the other. e.g. septate desmosome.

(iii) **Synaptic Desmosomes :** Provide low resistance to the passage of ions between cytoplasms of two otherwise separated cells, jointed by the desmosomes.

(E) According to the relation between the membranes of two cell surface areas involved in desmosomes of a pair :

(i) **Dismembranal Desmosomes :** The participating cell membranes are separated by an appreciable intercellular interval, which nevertheless, contains materials binding the two cell surfaces together.

(ii) **Juxtamembranal Desmosomes :** The cell membranes are very closely and intimately opposed in a parallel array but yet not fused with each other.

(iii) **Synmembranal Desmosomes :** The cell membranes are fused. It includes septate, syncytial and juxtalaminar desmosomes.

(F) According to the relations of the cytoplasm of the two participating cells :

(i) **Apocytical Desmosomes :** Those in which the cytoplasm of the two participating cells are completely separated by membrane of high electrical resistance and are not electrically coupled.

(ii) **Haptocytical Desmosomes :** Cytoplasm of two cells is completely separated by membrane of low electrical resistance and is electrically coupled.

(iii) **Syncytial Desmosomes :** There is no membrane between two cells. Some plasmodesmata represent this type. These are also filamentous and non-filamentous desmosomes in which tonofibrils are present in former forms and tonofibrils are absent in later case.

2.4.3 Plasmodesmata

Sometimes the cells are connected by bridges of cytoplasm passing between pores of cell wall or plasma membrane between the adjacent cells, such connections are called *plasmodesmata* (singular-plasmodesma). They are usually simple but anastomosing plasmodesmata may also found. Their number and distribution vary considerably. Like gap junctions, plasmodesmata provide intercellular channels for molecules of about 1000 molecular weight including a variety of metabolic and signalling compounds. These structures are prominant in plant cells and depending on the plant type the density of plasmodesmata varies from 1 to 10 per/μm^2.

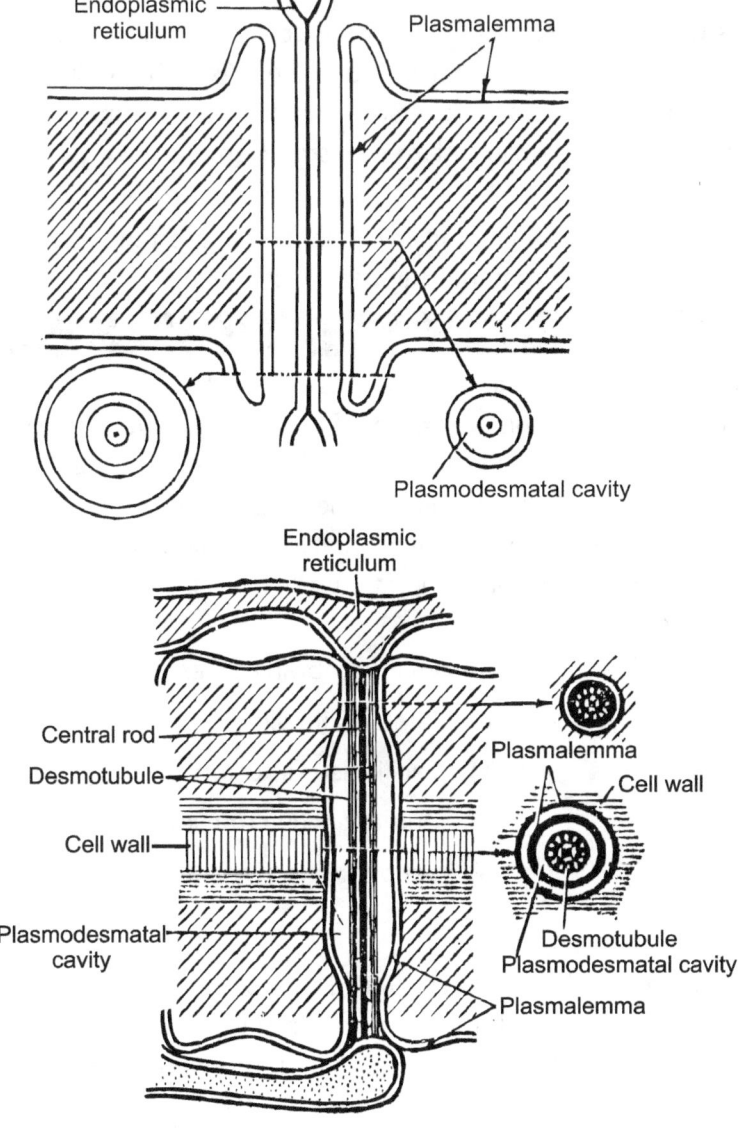

Fig. 2.15 : Plasmodesmata

Electron micrographs of plasmodesma show that it is a roughly cylindrical, membrane lined channel with a diameter of 20 to 60 nm and it traverses cell walls upto 90 nm thick. Plasmodesmata is a narrow cylindrical structure called desmotubule. The desmotubule is continuous with elements of endoplasmic reticulum membrane of each of the connected cells.

Between the outside of the desmotubules and the inner face of the cylindrical plasma membrane is an annulus of cytosol. It is constricted at each end of the plasmodesma. These constrictions may regulate the flux of molecules through the annulus that joins the two cytosols.

The plasmodesmata are needed in cell to cell communication. Many normal metabolic product such as sucrose are transported from cell to cell. As with gap junctions, movement of molecules through plasmodesmata is reversibly inhibited by an increase in cytosolic Ca^{2+}. Certain plant viruses and viroids can enlarge plasmodesmata in order to use this route to pass from cell to cell.

Through the plasmodesmata, cytoplasmic continuity is often maintained between the adjacent cells. Through them the material can pass from cell to cell.

2.5 TRANSPORT : PASSIVE AND ACTIVE

The main function of the plasma membrane is to regulate the flow of material into and out of the cell called transport. This transport of material is regulated by the size of pores present in the plasma membrane. Plasma membrane is semi-permeable which allows the passage of a solvent but not of all solute. The plasma membrane, which permits one substance to pass through more easily than another is called selectively permeable and it allows the passage of both solvent and solute. This plasma membrane is selectively permeable rather than semi-permeable.

Transport of metabolites through plasma membrane takes place in four ways :

(1) Passive Transport :   (i)   Simple diffusion

                              (ii) Facilitated diffusion

(2) Active Transport :   (i)   Primary active transport

                              (ii) Secondary active transport

2.5.1 Passive Transport

(1) Simple Diffusion : The simplest way for a solute to get from one side of the membrane to the other is simple diffusion. It is the unassisted net movement of a solute from a region where its concentration is higher to a region where its concentration is lower and concentration gradient disappears as diffusion occurs. There is no stereo specificity and it is slow process. ATP is not utilized.

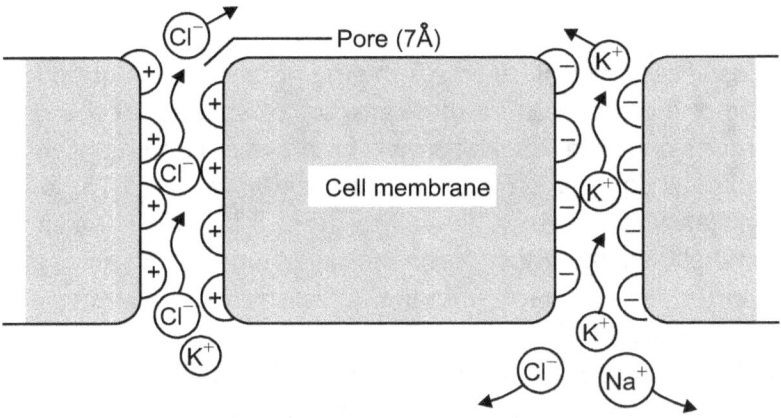

Fig. 2.16 : Simple Diffusion

(2) Facilitated Diffusion : In this type of diffusion, energy is not required and it takes place along the concentration gradient. However, it differs from simple diffusion in some respects, (i) It requires carrier for transport of the metabolite across the membrane. (ii) It is a stero specific process i.e. only one isomer is transported.

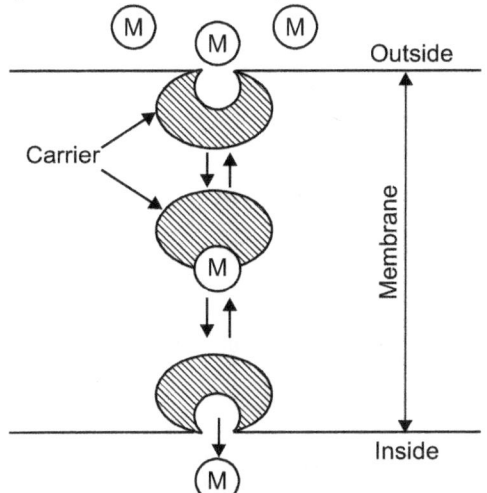

Fig. 2.17 : Facilitated Diffusion

The role of carrier protein is simply to facilitate the diffusion of a polar or changed solute. Carriers are proteins with relatively low molecular weight (9 to 40,000) but they are highly selective. The metabolite binds to the carrier protein at the outer surface of the membrane to form carrier metabolite complex. This diffuses along the concentration gradient i.e. from high concentration to low concentration regions.

Then metabolite is released towards the inner surface of the membrane as there is low concentration of metabolites on the inner side. It is continued as long as there is a concentration gradient. The transport of glucose into the erythrocytes is the good example of facilitated diffusion.

2.5.2 Active Transport

Diffusion of substances takes place across the membrane from high to low concentration. But membranes are also able to effect the transport of solutes up the gradient i.e. in the direction of increasing concentration. Normally, cells have a higher concentration of K^+ ions, which is maintained at all times when the cell is at resting potential. To do so, the cell has to continuously translocate a solute or K^+ ions into the cell by active transport mechanism at the expense of metabolic energy. Most of the inorganic ions, amino acids and carbohydrates are actively transported across the membrane. Cells always translocate essential nutrients outside to inside, irrespective of the concentration in the external medium.

This is essential in order to maintain a steady state. In many cells, equilibrium of diffusion can be adjusted by coupling energy yielding reactions, so that the cells are able to transloate solutes or metabolites against the concentration gradient. In addition, it allows various substances, such as secretary products and waste materials, to be removed from the cell or organelle even when their concentration outside is greater than that inside the cell. Third, it enables the cell to maintain constant, non-equilibrium intracellular concentrations of specific inorganic ions, notably K^+, Na^+, Ca^{++} and H^+.

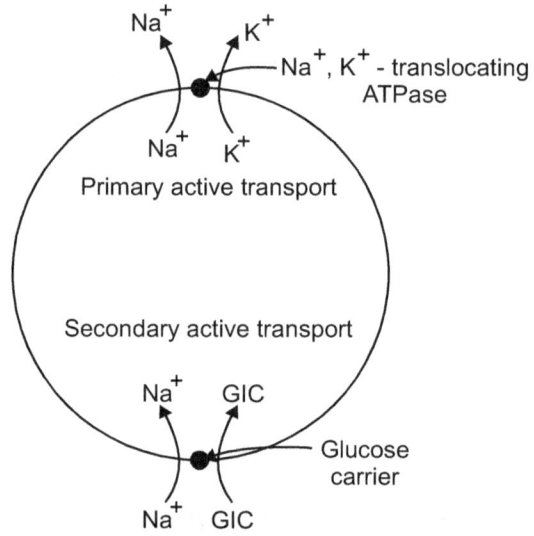

Fig. 2.18 : Active Transport

The membrane proteins involved in active transport are often called pumps which selectively transport specific components, molecules or ions from one fluid mass to another. The important features of active transport is that it has directionality. An active transport system that transports a solute across a membrane in one direction will not transport that solute actively in the other direction. Active transport is therefore said to be *unidirectional* or *vectorial* process.

Depending on the energy source, active transport is regarded as being either direct or indirect. In direct active transport, the accumulation of solute molecules or ions on one side of the membrane is coupled directly to an exergonic chemical reaction, most commonly the hydrolysis of ATP. Transport proteins driven directly by ATP hydrolysis are called transport ATPases or ATPase pumps.

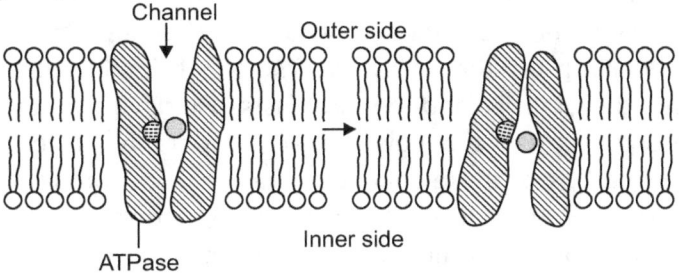

Fig. 2.19 : Another Model of the Functioning of Na⁺, K⁺, ATPase

Indirect active transport on the other hand, depends on the co-transport of the two solutes, with the movement of one solute down its gradient driving the movement of the other solute up its gradient.

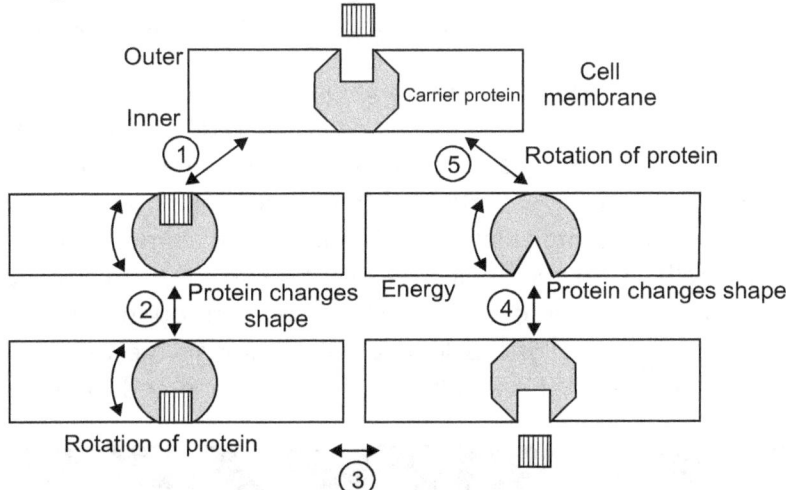

Fig. 2.20 : The Revolving Door Model of Active Transport

In most cases, one of the two solutes is an ion (usually Na^+ or H^+) that moves exergonically down its electrochemical gradient driving the concomitant transport of the second solute such as a mono-saccharide or amino acid against its concentration gradient.

Cell membranes allow water and non-polar molecules to penetrate by simple physical diffusion. However, cell membranes are permeable to various polar molecules, such as ions, sugars, amino acids, nucleotides, and many cell metabolites that pass across artificial lipid bilayers very slowly. It is now known that specific membrane proteins are responsible for transferring such solutes across cell membranes. These proteins referred to as membrane transport proteins, occur in many forms and in all the types of biological membranes.

Some transport proteins simply transport one solute from one side of the membrane to the other, they are called *uniports*. Others function as co-transport systems, in which the transfer of one solute depends on the simultaneous or sequential transfer of a second solute, either in the same direction is called symport or in the opposite direction is called *antiport*.

2.6 PINOCYTOSIS

Intake of fluid material into the cell by the formation of pinocytic *vesicles* or pinosomes is called pinocytosis. (Greek Pinetin-to drink) and has been described first by Lewis (1931). It is a kind of cellular drinking by the cell. This mode of intake of nutrients has been demonstrated in endothelial cells and erythroblasts. Fluids in contact with the plasma membrane move through narrow channels formed temporarily as deep invaginations into the cell interior. From the tips of these channels small vesicles containing the fluid droplets are budded off, which empty their contents in the cytoplasm. The vesicles are called pinosomes. Pinocytosis is found prominently in protozoa and best studied in amoeba. In amoeba, periodic pinocytosis has been observed under light microscope.

The process of pinocytosis is said to be mediated by some kind of inducer mechanism, which triggers the formation of invaginations in the plasma membrane.

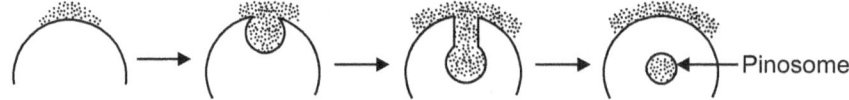

Fig. 2.21 : Process of Pinocytosis

Proteins in solution may act as good inducers as compared to acidic substances like DNA, RNA and fatty acids. All the substances surrounding the cell membrane may not be engulfed, hence the process is highly selective. Surface of the plasma membrane has specific receptor sites, to which only certain materials may be bound and carried through invaginating channels. Endothelial cells lining the capillaries may be cited to prove this point. Materials from the blood are transported into the interstitial space through small vesicles that are formed at the cell border. These vesicles loaded with materials are then transferred to the other side of the cell, where they fuse with the cell membrane and discharge the contents outside.

2.7 PHAGOCYTOSIS

Engulfment of solid particles with the help of plasma membrane has been observed in variety of cells such as leucocytes, endothelial cells, fibrocytes and spleenocytes.

The cell ingests or swallows foreign bodies, bacteria, harmful matter and other inert substances and the process is called phagocytosis. (Greek Phagein = to eat, kytos = cell).

It is found commonly in protozoans and among certain cells of metazoans. Phagocytosis has been observed in *Amoeba* for obtaining nutrition. The phagocytic cells in tissues of mammals are generally called macrophages, which are either mononucleate or multinucleate and distributed in a variety of mammalian tissues. The particles become absorbed (adheres) at the surface of membrane and later on they are taken into the cytoplasm by infolding of the plasma membrane which are soon pinched off forming vesicles consisting of particles enveloped by a membrane. These vesicles are called intracellular vesicles or phagosomes. The phagosome fuses with a primary lysosome to form a secondary lysosome in which food material is digestd by acidic enzymes.

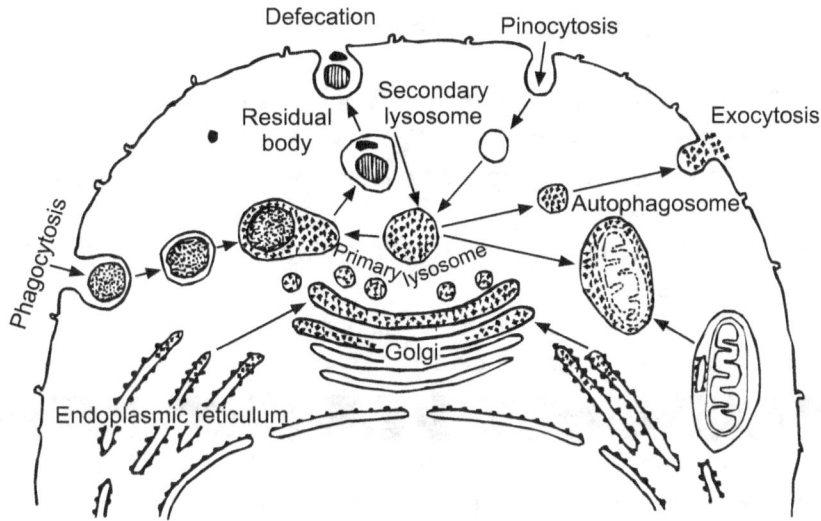

Fig. 2.22 : Phagocytosis

In metazoan, it is a method of defense against foreign bodies like bateria, dust and various colloids. Ingestion of small colloidal particles is called ultraphagocytosis.

During the process of phagocytosis, a number of events are observed. When there is material near phagocyte, the cell relays a signal to other cell to make presence known. Once signal is relayed other phagocytes pick it up and start moving towards the material to be engulfed. Exact nature is not known, but it is presumed that there is some kind of chemical interaction called chemotaxis between cell and the particulate material. They act on the macrophage surface to mediate a response.

Points to Remember

- The plasma membrane regulates what enters and leaves the cell.
- The plasma membrane is made up of lipoproteins.
- The plasma membrane contains integral and peripheral proteins.
- Carbohydrates of plasma membrane are in the form of glycolipids and glycoproteins.
- The fluid mosaic model proposed by Singer and Nicolson is the most accepted model for plasma membrane.
- The narrow invaginations or finger like projections of plasma membrane at the cell surface are known as microvilli.
- Caveolae are cave like invaginations of the cell surface.
- Tight junctions are located at the distal region between the adjacent cells where actual fusion of the outer membrane of the adjoining cells occurs.
- Gap junctions are called as communicating junctions located at specialized region of contact between opposed plasma membranes of the adjacent cells.
- Desmosomes are abundant in cells of skin, heart muscle, and the neck of the uterus.
- Desmosomes form early in embryonic development and play an important role in maintaining cell position during development.

- Tonofilaments are filaments anchor to the cell surface and tend to converge upon the desmosomes.
- Cytoskeleton fibres extend throughout the cell and form inter connections between the cell membrane and cell organelles.
- Plasmodesmata are bridges of cytoplasm passing between pores of cell wall or plasma membrane between the adjacent cells.
- Transport of metabolites through plasma membrane takes place either by passive transport or active transport.
- The cell ingests or swallows foreign bodies, bacteria, harmful matter and other inert substances by a process called phagocytosis.

Exercise

1. What is the significance of plasma membrane?
2. Describe the ultra structure, chemical composition and functions of plasma membrane.
3. With a neat and labelled diagram explain the fluid mosaic model of plasma membrane.
4. Describe in brief functions of plasma membrane.
5. Explain mechanism of pinocytosis, phagocytosis and active transport through plasma membrane.
6. Give a brief account of fluid mosaic model of plasma membrane.
7. Explain difference between pinocytosis and phagocytosis.
8. Write short notes.
   (a) Active transport   (b) Passive transport
   (c) Pinocytosis   (d)
   (e) Phagocytosis   (f) Fluid mosaic model
   (g) Functions of plasma membrane   (h) Membrane receptors
   (i) Microvilli   (j) Desmosomes
9. Define plasma membrane. Discuss its structure, chemistry and functions.
10. Which is the most accepted model of plasma membrane? Add a note on functions of plasma membrane.
11. Define membrane receptors and add a note on the mobile hypothesis on fluidity of the membrane.
12. Describe the modifications of plasma membrane.
13. Differentiate the following:
    a. Active and Passive transport
    b. Pinocytosis and Phagocytosis
    c. Cell wall and Plasma membrane
    d. Gap junction and Tight junction
    e. Simple diffusion and Facilitated diffusion

Chapter 3...

ENDOPLASMIC RETICULUM

- CONTENTS -

The endoplasmic reticulum is found in almost all animal and plant cells except erythrocytes and prokaryocytes. It was discovered by **Granier** in 1897. It is a network of double membrane, distributed extensively throughout the cytoplasm. **Porter (1961)** stated "the endoplasmic reticulum is a complex, finely divided vascular system, extending from the nucleus throughout the cytoplasm to the margin of the cell".

3.1 MORPHOLOGY

The endoplasmic reticulum occurs in three main forms, cisternae tubules and vesicles. The cisternae are broad, flattered, membrane bound spaces about 40 to 50 mµ thick and often arranged in parallel stacks. They are interconnected with each other. Tubules are more diverse in their shapes than cisternae. Their diameter ranges from 50 to 100 mm. Vesicles are rounded in shape and vary from 20 to 500 µm in diameter. Three forms of endoplasmic reticulum may appear in a single cell at the same time or may appear at different times during the cell cycle.

3.2 TYPES OF ENDOPLASMIC RETICULUM

There are two basic morphological types of the endoplasmic reticulum : (1) the rough endoplasmic reticulum or granular form and (2) the smooth endoplasmic reticulum or agranular form. The rough endoplasmic reticulum is so called because the membranes are covered with ribosomes, which give them a rough appearance. The smooth endoplasmic reticulum membranes are not covered with ribosomes.

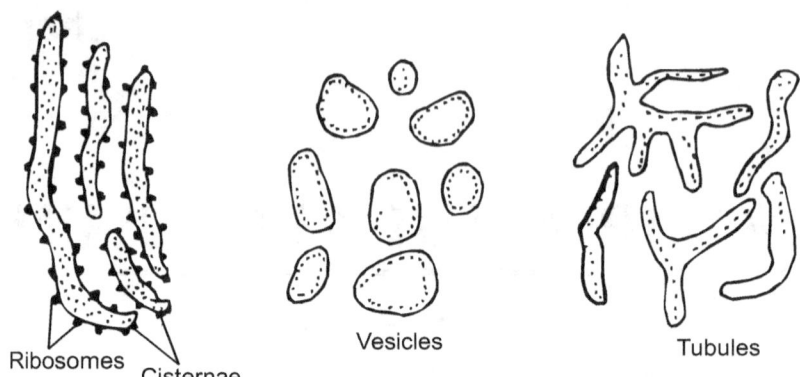

Ribosomes Cisternae   Vesicles   Tubules

Fig. 3.1 : Types of the endoplasmic reticulum

The Rough Endoplasmic Reticulums (RER) are extensively developed in the cells which actively synthesize proteins, e.g. enzymes secreting cells, while Smooth Endoplasmic Reticulum (SER) is characteristic of cells in which synthesis of non-protein substances like phospholipids, glycolipids, and steroid hormone takes place, e.g. adipose tissue cells, adrenocortical cells and interstitial cells of the testis.

The smooth ER is less stable than rough ER. The granular ER is involved in protein synthesis but the agranular ER has many functions other than protein synthesis. The ER membrane divides the cell into atleast two compartments. Secretory products, pinocytic material, phagocytic material are found in the compartment enclosed by the membranes.

A modified form of smooth ER is the sarcoplasmic reticulum found in striated muscles. The myeloid body in the pigment cells of the retina of the frog is possibly modified smooth ER. It consists of a number of tubules packed over one another. Myeloid bodies are light-sensitive regions in the cell and play an important role in photoreception.

Microsomes are not the normal structural units of the cells, but represent a functional unit. When cells are ground or homogenized the cell membrane breaks into fragments. The fragments then round off to bodies called microsomes. They are mostly fragments of ER. Under electron microscope they appear as a membrane bound vesicles, 500 to 1000A° diameter. This fraction contains most of the RNA (50 to 60% RNA of the cell) and phospholipids of the cell and shows high rate of protein synthesis than in non-ribosomal endoplasmic reticulum. The microsome is a heterogenous fraction containing not only the endoplasmic reticulum, but may also containing Golgi membrane, ruptured plasma membrane and other cell fragments.

The lipid content of microsomes is estimated to be 30-50% of which about 70% is phospholipids; 50-90% of the phospholipid content is in the form of lecithin and cephalin. The ER membrane has the typical three layered unit-membrane structure in some region, while in other region, it may show a globular (micellar) structure. It thus appears to have a combination of tripled layer and micellar structures.

3.3 FUNCTIONS OF ENDOPLASMIC RETICULUM

1. Mechanical Support : The endoplasmic reticulum divides the fluid content of cell into compartments and thus provides additional mechanical support for the colloidal structure of the cytoplasm. These compartments make possible the existence of ionic gradients and electrical potentials along ER membranes.

2. Cellular Metabolism : The membrane of the reticulum provides an increased surface for metabolic activities within the cytoplasm, such as synthesis of cholesterol, triglycerides and other lipids, indicating their probable role in lipid metabolism.

3. Protein Synthesis : The rough ER is the site of secretion of secretary proteins. Proteins are synthesized on the ribosomes and enter ER cisternae through channels in the membrane. It has been pointed out that the free ribosomes are not as active in protein synthesis as are those associated with ER. This suggests that the membrane contributes in some way to the efficiency of the process.

In pancreatic aciner cells of the dog, dense granules are seen in the cisternae. In the liver cell of salamander *Bairachoseps attenuates* protein crystals have been found in the granular cisternae. Thus the ER has a property similar to that of the Golgi complex, namely *concentration of products* into dense granules.

4. Intracellular Transport : Protein including enzymes, lipids and probably other materials, are transported and distributed to the various parts of the cell through ER. In some cases, these materials may accumulate and may be stored within the ER for considerable time.

5. Detoxification : Smooth ER is also involved in the detoxification of many endogenous and exogenous compounds. Prolonged administration of certain drugs (phenobarbital) results in the increased activity of enzymes related to detoxification, as well as other enzymes and a considerable hypertrophy of the smooth ER.

6. Membrane Flow : Transport of ions, molecules and particles into and out of the cells may also take place through membrane flow. Thus, substances like RNA and nuclear proteins may pass out from the nucleus to the outside of the cell by the following route :

Nuclear membrane → Pores → ER → Golgi complex → Plasma membrane → Outside. Particles enter the cell by a reverse membrane involving pinocytosis/phagocytosis by the plasma membrane and vesicle formation i.e. endocytosis.

7. Ionic Gradients : The sarcoplasmic reticulum of striated muscle is involved in the concentration of calcium ions by an energy utilizing ATP. The calcium ions are stored in the sarcoplasmic reticulum. When the muscle is stimulated by nerve impulses, hormone or other means, the calcium ions are released, leading to muscular *contraction*.

8. Formation of Plasmodesmata : Electron microscopic studies suggest that the endoplasmic reticulum in plants plays a special role in the interconnection of cells through the cytoplasmic strands called plasmodesmata.

9. Formation of Secondary Wall : In the formation of secondary cell wall in plants, certain enzymes and metabolites may be carried by the reticulum to the region of wall synthesis.

10. Glycogen Synthesis and Storage : Residual glycogen has been found associated with the endoplasmic reticulum in fasting animals. On resumption of feeding, there is an increase in the endoplasmic reticulum glycogen.

The enzyme glucose-6-phosphatase has been reported in the ER of rat liver cells. It has been linked to breakdown of glycogen (glycogenolysis). It has been also suggested that the SER membranes play a role in the synthesis of glycogen (glycogenesis).

11. Lipid Synthesis and Storage : Electron microscopic and autoradiographic studies of Stein and Stein (1967) suggested that the ER was the site of triglyceride formation. They injected radioactive labelled material (3H-palmitate and 3H-glycogen) into fasted ethanol treated rats. It was found that the labelled material was seen in the SER and RER after two minutes. Claude (1970) has suggested that triglyceride synthesis may be limited to the SER, while protein and perhaps phospholipids are synthesized in the RER.

The SER membrane also appear to be involved in the formation of lipoprotein complexes. The SER is also implicated in the initial stages of the breakdown of fatty acids. Conversion of fatty acid to acetyl coenzyme A esters occurs mainly in the ER.

The ER has been associated with the storage of lipids. When starved rats were fed with corn oil, the oil droplets first appeared in pinocytic vesicles, below the microvilli of intestinal epithelial cells. After about an hour, the lipid was found in the ER and the Glogi complex. Thus, the ER appears to have a general role in the intracellular and storage of lipids.

12. Synthesis of Cholesterol and Steroid Hormones : Cholesterol is an important precursor of steroid hormones. The major site of cholesterol synthesis is the ER. In rats, injected with radioactively labelled acetate, nearly all the labelled cholesterol is found in the microsomal fraction. The microsomes have also been shown to be the principal sites of cholesterol forming enzymes. The intermediates *squalene* and *lanosterol* in cholesterol synthesis are bound to the ER in rat liver cells. In liver cells, the SER is believed to be concerned with both the synthesis and storage of cholesterol.

In the testis, ovary and the adrenal cortex, the SER has a role in the synthesis of steroid hormones. A well developed SER has been demonstrated in the interstitial cells of the testis of the opossum and the guinea pig (Christensen 1965). The enzyme catalyzing biosynthesis of androgens have been located in the SER. There is a strong correlation between the amounts of SER in cells and the capacity to synthesize steroid hormones.

13. Formation of Microbodies : Closely related with the ER are microbodies, which are small granular bodies filled with an electron dense substance and limited by a single membrane. They have been found in the protozoa, yeast, higher plants, liver and kidney. In rat liver cells there are 70 - 100 microbodies with an average diameter of 0.6 to 0.7 μm. Microbodies are formed as dilations of the ER and frequently show connection with the ER cisternae. They are rich in enzyme peroxidase (and are hence also called peroxisomes), catalase, and D-amino acid oxidase. In plant cells, the enzymatic content is different, and the bodies are glyoxysomes because they include enzymes of the glyoxylate cycle.

Peroxisomes produce oxidative enzymes which generate hydrogen peroxide (H_2O_2). The enzymes are *urate oxidase, D-amino oxidase* and *a-hydroxylic acid oxidase.* They produce hydrogen peroxide which is toxic to the cell. Another enzyme produced is *catalase* which destroys hydrogen peroxide, and therefore probably plays a protective role. Peroxide shows a relationship with steroid synthesis and generation of NAD and NADPH.

14. Origin of Cell Organelles : There are also evidences to show that ER is the place for the origin of the organelles known as primary lysosomes.

15. Amphibian Development : There are evidences to suggest that the ER contributes in several ways to the development of the amphibian embryo.

16. Cell Differentiation : Some specific instances of a development have been studied in detail, which more or less confirm the contention that the ER is important in the process of cell differentiation. Not only this much, ER also plays a role in co-ordinating the differentiation.

Points to Remember

- Endoplasmic reticulum is an interconnected network of membrane vesicles.
- Two basic morphological types of the endoplasmic reticulum (1) the rough endoplasmic reticulum or granular form and (2) the smooth endoplasmic reticulum or agranular form.
- The rough ER is involved in protein synthesis while the smooth ER has functions other than protein synthesis.
- The Endoplasmic reticulum is found in almost all animals and plants except matured crythrocytes and prokaryocytes. It was discovered by Granier in 1897.
- It is occurs in three main forms, cisternae, tubules and vesicles. It may be appear in single cells at the same time or may appear at different times during the cell cycle.
- There are two basic morphological types of the endoplasmic reticulum (1) the rough endoplasmic reticulum (RER) and (2) Smooth endoplasmic reticulum (SER).
- It helps in Mechanical support, cellular metabolism, protein synthesis, intracellular transport, detoxification etc.

Exercise

1. Give an account of ultra structure of endoplasmic reticulum and describe its functions in brief.

2. Describe various types of ER. Enumerate the common and specialized functions of smooth endoplasmic reticulum.

3. Describe the position and structure of various types of ER. Explain its functions.

4. Differentiate between rough and smooth endoplasmic reticulum.

5. Mention the function of Endoplasmic Reticulum.

6. Describe the morphology and functions of ER.

7. Define rough and smooth endoplasmic reticulum. Add a note on its physiological significance.

GOLGI COMPLEX

- CONTENTS -

4.1 GOLGI COMPLEX

Golgi complex was first discovered by **Golgi**, an Italian neurologist in 1898 who named it "natural reticular apparatus". Various names have been given to this organelle by various workers. **Baker** (1951, 1953) referred to the Golgi complex as lipochondria because of the presumed lipid content. Structures similar to the Golgi complex have been found in plants. Botanists refer to them as *dictyosomes*.

The term Golgi complex has been preferred because of the following reasons :

(1) Electron microscopy demonstrates fairly discrete groups of lamellar units.

(2) Perroncito had earlier established a definite use for dictyosomes.

(3) Each dictyosome appears to function in membrane building, product synthesis and assembly, and in the evolution of products as an individual organelle.

4.1.1 Morphology

The shape of Golgi is quite variable in somatic animal cells; even in the same cell, there are variation with functional stages. In some cases, it occurs as a dense reticulum of anastomosing trabeculae while in others, as an irregular lenestrated plaque, or hollow spheres united together. In nerve cells, it occurs as a reticulum of wide meshes around the nucleus.

The size of the Golgi is also variable. It is small in muscle cells but quite large in the nerve cells and gland cells.

The number of Golgi apparatus per cell is also variable. Some cells have been recorded as having a single apparatus, other cells with dispersed Golgi apparatus may have hundreds. Some glandular cells having only a single apparatus but of appreciable extent.

The position of Golgi is relatively fixed for each cell type. In the cells which are ectodermal in origin, the Golgi is polarised and is present between the nucleus and the periphery of the cell. In the secondary exocrine gland, it is generally found between the nucleus and the excretory pore. In the endocrine gland cells, its polarity is variable except in thyroid, where it is oriented towards the centre of the follicle.

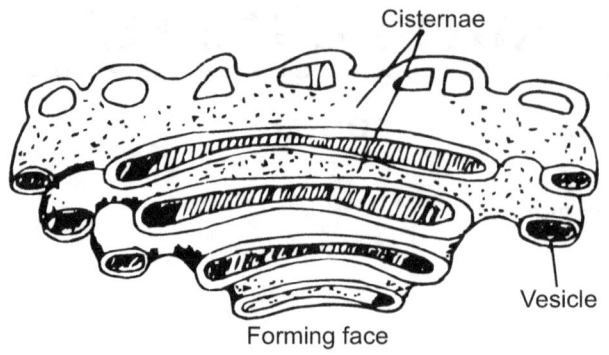

(A) Sterocopic View

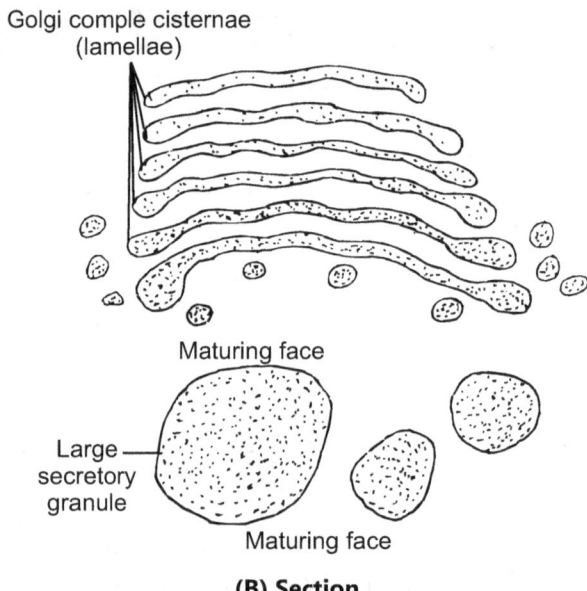

(B) Section

Fig. 4.1 : Golgi Complex

4.2 STRUCTURE

The first electron micrograph of Golgi complex was proposed by Dalton and Felix, 1954. They described the Golgi complex in the epididymis of the rat as consisting of three components; flattened sacs or cisternae, large vacuoles and small granules. These are all membranous structures and are characterised by the absence of ribosomes i.e. they are smooth membranes.

The cisternae or lamellae are the most constant elements of the Golgi complex. They consist of flattened, parallel sacs situated one upon the other to form stacks. The number of cisternae in a stack varies from species to species and sometimes from one developmental stage to another. The number of cisternae in a stack is about 4 to 5 in most animal and plant cells. In *Euglena*, the number may go up to 20. The membrane of cisternae is roughly 70 A° in thickness which encloses a cavity about 150 A° wide whose edges are often dilated.

According to Mollenhauer and Whaley 1963, in certain plant cells the Golgi complex is polarized and has two well defined faces "forming faces and maturing face". The forming or proximal face is the outer side, while the maturing or distal face is on the opposite side. It is also possible that a lamella of the ER buds off vesicles, which then become arranged on the forming face of the ER and may be converted into a Golgi lamella by loss of ribosomes. On the other side, is a maturing or secreting face, where the lamella buds off secretory vesicles. Thus, new lamellae are formed on the forming face and maturing lamellae are lost on the maturing face. The cisternae lie parallel to each other and are separated from each other by a space at about 200 to 300 A°. Chemical composition shows that, Golgi complex membrane is intermediate between those of ER and the plasmalemma. The membranes at the forming face of the Golgi complex are similar to the ER membrane and those of the maturing face, to the plasmalemma. The membranes of the Golgi complex are in dynamic equilibrium. They are continually receiving lammellae through budding off of vesicles from the smooth ER and losing membranes through formation of secretory vesicles.

In a few cases, dense material has been found between the cisternae of the Golgi complex and has been called intercisternal material. The composition and function of the intercisternal material is not known. It has been suggested that it acts as a cementing substance, holding the cisterntae together.

Vesicles

The small vesicles are 400 to 800 A° in diameter. They are intimately associated with the cisternae and may show continuity with them. The small vesicles arise from the cisternae by budding or pinching off.

The large vacuoles are clear and generally lie at the edge of the Golgi complex. They represent modified and expanded cisternae in which the two membranes have become widely separated and the vacuolar space enlarged. They contain clear material which reduce metallic salts.

Chemical Composition

Morphologically, Golgi complex lies between the ER and plasma membrane, the three membrane being linked by transitional structures and by secretory granules. This suggest that the Golgi complex membrane are in the intermediate state of differentiation between ER membrane and the plasma membrane. Generally, it consists of about 60% protein and 40% lipid; some proteins being common to those found in ER, but having fewer protein bonds. Very low level of RNA, DNA and polysaccharides have been noted in some Golgi functions.

The natural lipid fraction contains mainly cholesterol, cholesterol esters and triglycerides. The enzyme concentrated in the Golgi fraction comprises thiamine pyrophosphatase and several glycosyl transferase.

4.3 FUNCTIONS

1. Golgi and Cell Secretion / Role in Secretion: There are definite evidences which suggest relationship between Golgi and cell secretion which was postulated by Cajal, 1914. The very fact that, the Golgi are very well developed in all the cells exhibiting high secretory activity, clearly suggest that they play main role in the formation of secretion granules.

Many electron microscope studies shows that during vitellogenesis in oocytes, yolk products first become visible in the cisternae of Golgi complex. However, in these studies it is not clear whether the yolk actually synthesizes the Golgi complex or only packs them. In certain oocytes, the Golgi complex appears to give rise to critical granules.

In some cells, formed products appear in the expanded end of the Golgi lamillae. In others, secretory products completely fill the cisternae. The secretory products within the Golgi lamellae are very similar to the contents of the secretory granules near the Golgi complex. In some cases, the ends of the Golgi cisternae may be pinched off to form small secretory granules. These may then fuse to form large granules. In other cases, the individual cisternae on the "mature face" may be completely filled with secretory products and then become rounded to form secretory granules. New cisternae would then apparently be formed on the forming face. It is possible that the ER may become Golgi lamellae by loss of ribosomes.

2. Role in Protein Secretion : In pancreatic exocrine cells, the distribution of secretory proteins (digestive enzymes) has been investigated by Siekevitz, Palade in 1962.

(a) Proteins are formed on the ribosomes attached to the ER.

(b) These nascent proteins are then transferred into the ER.

(c) From here, they go to the Golgi complex. There is morphological evidence that the ER may bud off vesicles which travel towards the Golgi complex. The vesicle may then fuse with the membrane of the Golgi cisternae and release their content into the latter.

(d) In the Golgi complex, the proteins are concentrated and transformed into zymogen granules. The zymogen of the granules consists of enzyme precursor of the pancreatic juice. The membrane of the Golgi vacuole becomes the limiting membrane of the zymogen granules.

(e) The zymogen granules released from the Golgi complex, migrate to the surface of the cell. Here the limiting membrane of zymogen granules fuses with the plasmalemma, thus discharging its contents. This process is a form of "reversed pinocytosis".

Thus, it is apparent that the Golgi complex acts as a condensation for proteins formed on the ribosomes. The concentrated material is then packed for secretion.

3. **Synthesis of Carbohydrates :** Golgi also synthesizes the carbohydrates.

(a) In plant cells, it has been demonstrated to produce pectic materials which are enclosed in vesicles, moves to the cell wall region. Here vesicle membrane fuses with the plasma membrane and the vesicle contents accumulate between the cell wall and the plasma membrane.

(b) Similar observations have been made in the formation of new cell plate at the time of cell division in plants. Abundant dictyosomes cut off vesicles, which move to the cell plate region and fuse together, releasing constituents of new cell plate.

4. **Enzymes** including acid have often been demonstrated to be active in dictyosomes. The most characteristic enzymes, associated with Golgi membrane, are those linking sugars with proteins to form glucoproteins, for example : mucopolysaccharide, used by hydra for attaching its base to the substratum.

5. Neutra and Leblond carried out autoradiographic studies to show that Golgi produces pectic substances. They proposed the following scheme for polysaccharide synthesis.

(a) Precursers enter the goblet cells from the capillaries of the vascular system.

(b) The amino acids are synthesized into proteins on the ribosomes of the ER.

(c) The proteins are then transferred to the cisternae of the Golgi complex.

(d) The simple sugar molecules go directly from the blood stream to the golgi complex cisternae, where they are complexed with protein to form glycoprotein.

(e) The glycoprotein is then sulphated in the golgi complex to form mucigen.

(f) The distal cisternae becomes rounded off and are transformed into mucigen granules.

(g) The mucigen granules are progressively displaced towards the apex of the cell. During this process, the mucigen undergoes further modification.

(h) The mucigen granules are secreted into the intestine by exocytosis during which the vesicle membrane fuses with the plasma membrane.

6. It takes an active part in the incorporation of substances from the environment.

7. **Formation of Acrosome during Spermatogenesis :** During the maturation of sperm, the Golgi plays a role in the formation of acrosome. In early stages, Golgi appear as a spherical body, comprising cisternae arranged in parallel stacks and numerous small vesicles. These are always pinched off from the cisternae. As development proceeds, the Golgi becomes irregular in shape and large vacuoles are formed by dilation of cisternae sacs. In the centre of these large vacuoles, are present dense granule and the proacrosomal granules. These granules seem to be the enlarging vacuole. This vacuole along with granules approaches the anterior pole of the nuclear membrane constituting acrosomal granule. With the elongation of the spermatid, the acrosomal vesicle spreads over the nuclear surface and finally collapses with the nuclear membrane, forming a cap material. The acrosomal granule

becomes the acrosome which lies at the apex of the nucleus and apparently comprises certain enzymes involved in the process of fertilization.

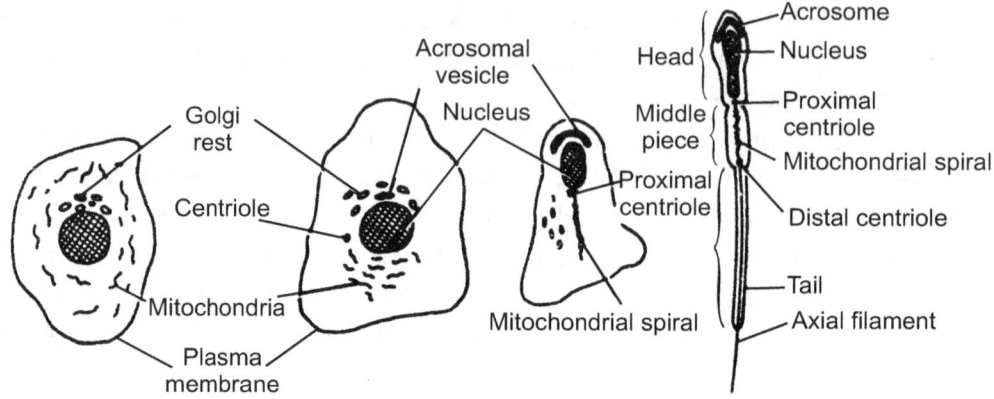

Fig. 4.2 : formation acrosome from Golgi Complex

8. Pigment Formation : In many mammalian tumour and cancer cells, the Golgi complex has been described as the site of origin of pigment granules (melanin). The Golgi complex has also been associated with pigment formation, in renal pigment epithelium of chick embryo, in the test cells of the ovaries of certain tunicates and in the oocytes of the Salamander.

Points to Remember

- Morphologically, Golgi complex lies between the ER and plasma membrane.
- The membranes of Golgi, ER and plasma membrane are linked by transitional structures and by secretary granules.
- The position of Golgi is relatively fixed for each cell type.
- Golgi complex was first discovered by Golgi in 1898.
- The Golgi apparatus is a system of roughly parallel interconnecting flattened sacs situated close to the endoplasmic reticulum but physiologically separate from them.
- It is helps in cell secretion, protein secretion, synthesis of carbohydrates, and pigments formation.

Exercise

1. Give an account of the structure and functions of the Golgi body or Golgi apparatus.
2. Describe the morphology, origin and chemical composition of Golgi complex.
3. Write short notes on:
   a. Morphology of Golgi complex
   b. Structure of Golgi complex
   c. Chemical composition of Golgi complex
   d. Functions of Golgi complex

LYSOSOMES

- CONTENTS -

The lysosomes were first isolated in 1949, as a class of cell particles having centrifugal properties intermediate between those of mitochondria and ribosomes. These particles were rounded, dense bodies observed in hepatic cells and first called *pericanalicular danse* bodies. In 1955, **de Duve** renamed these bodies as lysosomes (lyso = digestive; soma = body) because they contain digestive enzymes capable of lysis or digestion.

5.1 OCCURRENCE AND ORIGIN OF LYSOSOMES

The lysosomes may originate directly from the endoplasmic reticulum or from the Golgi membranes and then they associate with the vesicles formed by pinocytosis or phagocytosis. There is evidence that the lysosomes are also originated from the Golgi complex. The protein granules synthesized by the ribosomes are seen in the enlargements of endoplasmic reticulum. When these are budded off, give rise to bodies having properties of lysosomes. They are also formed by pinocytic vesicles.

Lysosomes have been found both in animal and plant cells and in protozoa. In bacteria, there are no lysosomes, but the so-called *periplasmic space,* found between plasma membrane and the cell wall, may play a role similar to that of the lysosomes.

5.2 STRUCTURE OF LYSOSOMES

It is difficult to identify the lysosomes under electron microscope because they have no characteristic shape or structure. They usually appear as a dense globular body and vary in size from 0.2 to 0.8 µ in diameter. They may be large in mammalian kidney (5 µ) and exceedingly large in phagocytes. The lysosome is essentially a sphere of single lipoprotein membrane containing hydrolytic enzymes; which are involved in the mechanisms of cellular digestion. If the enzymes are released, they can digest the cell. The membrane is impermeable to substrates of the enzymes contained in the lysosomes. The substances having molecular weight higher than 200 do not diffuse through the membrane. This indicates that lysosomal hydrolases have no direct access to cellular components which prevents uncontrolled digestion of the cell contents. Thus, lysosomal membrane is resistant to the enzymes that it encloses, and entire process of digestion is carried out within the lysosome. The enzymes have destructive effects on the rest of the cell, hence the stability of the membrane is of great importance to the normal function of the cell. In fact, pathological conditions are known in which this membrane becomes more labile and permits exit of the enzymes causing destruction of the cells. Another interesting point is that most of the lysosomal enzymes act in an acidic medium.

The identification of the lysosomes is possible with the use of electron microscope and various cytochemical techniques. The most widely used procedure is the Gomori stain for acid phosphatase. Cytochemical reactions for β-glucuronidase, aryl sulfatase, N-acetyl, β-glucosaminidase and 5 bromo 4-chloroindoleacetate - estarase can also stain the lysosomes. Certain substances like neutral red, antimalarial drugs, vitamin A are taken up by lysosomes and may be used in their identification.

5.2.1 Types of Lysosomes

The lysosomes are polymorphic. They show irregularities in size and internal structure. Because of polymorphic nature, lysosomes are extremely dynamic and this can be recognized after isolation of the lysosomes. When lysosomes are within the cell, they are surrounded by *multivesicular bodies,* smooth and coated vesicles and dense bodies. These bodies show fusion and fission events.

At present, four types of lysosomes are recognised of which only the first is *the primary lysosome,* the other three may be grouped together as *secondary lysosomes.*

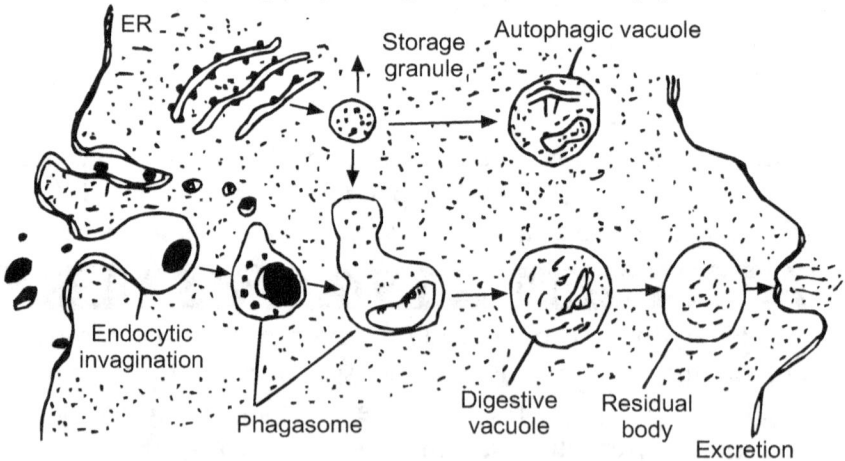

Fig. 5.1 : Different Types of Lysosomes and their Origin

(1) Primary lysosomes : They are also called storage granules. Each primary lysosome is small body and its enzymatic content is synthesized by the ribosomes and accumulated in the endoplasmic reticulum. From these the enzymes penetrate into the Golgi region, in which the first acid phosphatase reaction takes place. The primary lysosome may be charged preferentially with one type of enzyme or the other.

(2) Digestive vacuoles : They are also called heterophagosomes. They are formed by phagocytosis or pinocytosis of foreign material by the cell. These are secondary lysosome which contain the engulfed material within a membrane and shows positive acid phosphatase reaction. This may be due to fusion with primary lysosomes. They contain enzymes, and the material to be digested or already digested materials are present.

(3) Residual bodies : After digestion, the end products pass through the lysosomal membrane and are incorporated into the cell. The undigested material is left or if the digestion is incomplete the secondary lysosomes formed are called residual bodies. In some cells such as *Amoeba* and other protozoa, these residual bodies are eliminated. But in other cells, they remain for long and may load the cell.

(4) Autophagic vacuoles : These secondary lysosomes are also called cytolysosomes or autophagosomes. These are special types of lysosomes in which they contain a part of the cell in the process of digestion (e.g. a mitochondria or portions of endoplasmic reticulum). Lysosomes regularly engulf bits of cylosol, which is degraded by a mechanism called *microautophagy.* During starvation, the liver cells show numerous autophagic vacuoles. This is a mechanism by which the cell can achieve the degradation of its own constituents which have undergone irrepairable damage.

5.2.2 Lysosomal Enzymes

Lysosomes contain variety of enzymes upto the present time about 40 enzymes have been isolated. Some of the enzymes found in lysosomes are shown in table 5.1. Most of the enzymes function better under acidic condition (optimum pH - 5) and they are collectively called as *acid hydrolases.*

Table 5.1 : Some Acid Hydrolases of Lysosomes

	Enzyme	Natural Substrate	Source of Lysosomes
(a)	Nucelases Acid ribonuclease Acid deoxyribonuclease	RNA DNA	Many tissues of animals and plants.
(b)	Phosphatases Oligonucleotides	Most phosphomonoesters and phosphodiesters	Many tissues of animals and plants

	Acid Phosphodiesterase		
(c)	Proteases Cathepsin Collagenase Peptidases	Proteins Collagen Peptides	Animals Bone Animals and Plants
(d)	Lipases Esterases Phospholipases	Fatty acids esters Phospholipids	Animals and plants
(e)	Glycosidases β-Galactosidase α-Glucosidase β-Glucoronidase	Galactosides Glycogen Glycogen Mucopolysaccharides Polysaccharides	Liver
(f)	Lysozyme	Bacterial cell wall and kidney mucopolysaccharides	Egg white saliva
(g)	Hyaluronidase Arlysulphatase	Hyaluronic acids Chondroitin sulphates Organic sulphates	Liver Liver, Plants

The lysosomes degrade every biological macromolecules. A single lysosome need not contain all the enzymes. Many of the enzymes exist in multiple molecular forms.

5.3 FUNCTIONS OF LYSOSOMES

1. Intracellular digestion : It is the digestion which occurs inside the cell. The lysosomes contain enzymes and digest material intracellularly. Intracellular digestion is of two types : autophagy and heterophagy.

Autophagy is intracellular digestion in which enzymes of the cell digest the pieces of cytoplasmic material from the cell itself, i.e., digestion of endogenous material. Mitochondria are constantly removed by this process. Thus, there is renovation and turnover of cellular components.

Heterophagy means intake of exogenous material into the cell and its breakdown by lysosomal enzymes. Endocytosis is phenomenon in which bulk of exogenous material is taken inside the cell. It includes two phenomena, pinocytosis, i.e. incorporation of liquid material and phagocytosis i.e. intake of solid material.

2. Extracellular digestion : The lysosomal enzymes are also released outside the cell and they hydrolyse the extracellular material. Lysosomal enzymes also involved in bone erosion. Such process may occur in rheumatoid arthritis, a human disease in which the cartilage of the joints may be eroded by lysosomes.

3. Hormone secretion : The lysosomal proteases activate the secretion of thyroid hormones in the follicles.

4. Lysosomes are important in germ cells and fertilization : The acrosome of spermatozoan is nothing but a special lysosome which contains protease and hyaluronidase. These enzymes are useful for penetration of sperm into egg and also digestion of stored reserve materials.

5. Role in development processes : Many developmental processes involve the shedding or remodelling of tissues with the removal of whole cells and extracellular material. For example, the degeneration of the tadpole tail is produced by the action of cathepsins (i.e., proteolytic enzymes) contained in the lysosomes.

6. Lysosomes involved in human diseases and syndromes : In certain pathological conditions, such as rheumatoid arthritis, silicosis, and asbestosis (diseases produced by the inhalation of silica or asbestos particles) and gout (in which crystals of urate accumulate in the joints), there is a release of lysosomal enzymes from the macrophages and acute inflammation of the tissues that may lead to an increase in collagen synthesis (fibrosis). An acute release of lysosomal enzymes occur in states of anoxia, acidosis and shock, and results in increased amounts of enzymes in the blood. The lipid-soluble vitamins (A, K, D & E) and the steroid hormones make the membrane more susceptible to rupture. On the other hand, cortisone, hydrocortisone and other drugs have anti-inflammatory action, tend to stabilize the lysosomal membrane.

7. Storage diseases caused by mutations that affect lysosomal enzymes : Several congenital diseases have been found in which there is accumulation within the cells of substances such as glycogen or various glycolipids. These are called storage diseases and are produced by mutation that affects one of the lysosomic enzymes, involved in the catabolism of a certain substance. For example, in glycogenosis type II, the liver and muscles are filled with glycogen within membrane-bound organelles. In this disease α-glycosidase, the enzyme that degrades glycogen to glucose, is absent There are about 20 diseases due to lack of certain lysosomal enzymes.

8. Lysosomes in plant cells and their role in seed germination : Lysosomes are found in plant cells. In seedlings, they are involved in the hydrolysis and in removal of protein and starch during germination.

Points to Remember

- Lysosomes are rounded, dense bodies which contain digestive enzymes capable of lysis or digestion.

- Lysosomes originate directly from the endoplasmic reticulum or from the Golgi membranes.

- They bud off from the membranes and associate with the vesicles formed by pinocytosis or phagocytosis.

- Lysosomal membrane is resistant to the enzymes that it encloses.

- When lysosomes are within the cell, they are surrounded by multivesicular bodies which show fusion and fission events.

- Lysosomes have been found both in animal and plant cells and in protozoa but in bacteria, there are no lysosomes.

Exercise

1. Describe the structure and functions of lysosomes.
2. What are lysosomes? Describe origin, structure and functional significance.
3. Lysosomes are suicide bags in the cell. Explain.
4. Define Lysosomes. Describe their functions.
5. Define Lysosomes. How they can be regarded as polymorphic?
6. Differentiate
   a. Primary and secondary lysosomes
   b. Intracellular and Extracellular digestion

MITOCHONDRIA

- CONTENTS -

Mitochondria are small granular, filamentous bodies generally known as *"Powerhouse of the Cell"*, which are found in the cytoplasm of all aerobically respiratory cells of plants and animals, but not in bacteria where respiratory enzymes are located in the plasma membrane. Thus, they are associated with cellular respiration and are the sources of energy.

6.1 MORPHOLOGY AND BIOGENESIS

Mitochondria vary in shape but are generally granular or filamentous. They may swell out at one end to become club-shaped. They may become vesicular by the appearance of central clear zone. Polymorphic forms may contain swellings at both ends.

The size of mitochondria is also variable. The average length of the mitochondria is 3 to 4 μ and the average diameter 0.5 to 1.0 μ. The different physical and chemical factors such as pH, cell environment and the osmotic pressure influence the size and shape of mitochondria.

The number of mitochondria varies in different cell types. The number of mitochondria depends upon the metabolic activity of the cell. Cell with high metabolic activity have a high number of mitochondria, while those with low metabolic activity have a lower number. In giant amoeba *Chaos chaos* there may be 500,000 mitochondria. Large *sea-urchin* eggs have 13,000 to 14,000 while renal tubules have 300 to 400. They are fewer in green plant cells than in animal cells because some of their functions are taken over by chloroplast.

Generally, they are evenly distributed in the cytoplasm. In some cases, they are aggregated around the nucleus. In *Paramoecium*, they are located beneath the cell surface. During cell division, they accumulate about the spindle and upon division of the cell, are distributed more or less equally among the daughter cell. In skeletal muscles they lie between the myofibrils.

6.1.1 Mitochondrial Formation or Biogenesis

Regarding the origin of mitochondria or biogenesis four basic hypothesis are generally discussed.

(1) **De navo** origin of mitochondria.

(2) Mitochondrial formation from other intracellular structures.

(3) Formation by growth and division of pre-existing mitochondria.

(4) Prokaryotic origin of mitochondria or symbiont hypothesis.

(1) *De navo* origin of Mitochondria : *De navo* synthesis of mitochondria has been traced in a variety of cells. It is stipulated that cytoplasmic vesicles from **De navo**, accompanied by budding and membrane covering. The buds thus formed grow in size, followed by compartmentalization through vesicular formation, which ultimately develop into cristae. This hypothesis carry little weight today because the observations were made with light microscope.

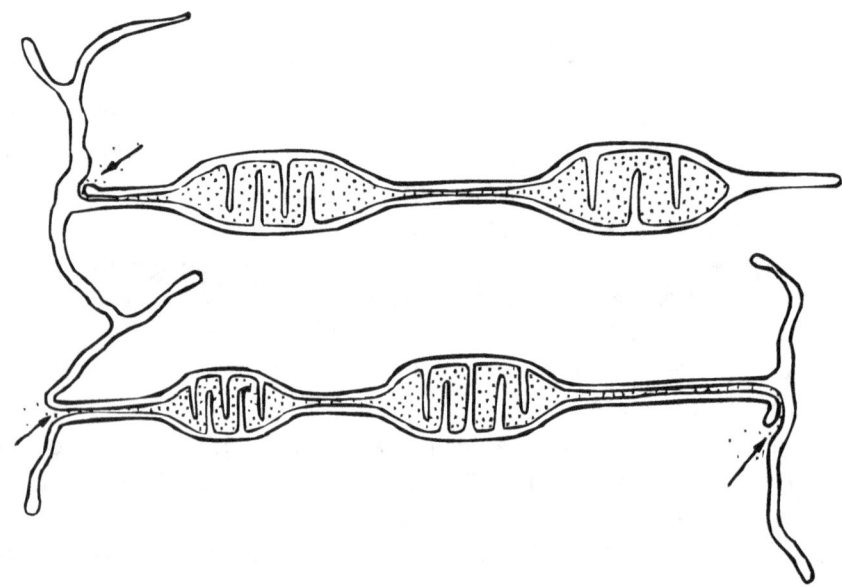

Fig. 6.1 : A Possible Mechanism for the Origin of Mitochondrion

(2) Mitochondrial Formation from other Intracellular Structures : In this case, the mitochondria are originated by invaginations of the cell membrane. According to **Green (1956)** and **Robert son (1964)** the protuberance passes into the invagination of cell membrane to form double membrane lined tubule which enlarges into a vesicle. Soon from the inner membrane several outgrowths arise to form cristae, thus forming mitochondrion. Endoplasmic reticulum might have given rise to mitochondrion. A finger-like invagination of cytoplasmic matrix extends into the cavity of large endoplasmic reticulum cisterna.

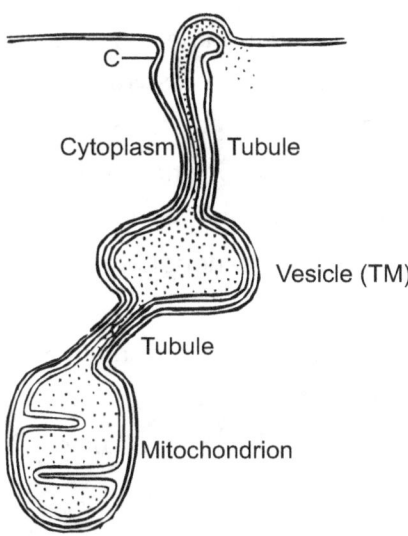

Fig. 6.2 : A Possible Mechanism for the Origin of Mitochondrion from Plasma Membrane

(3) Formation of Growth and Division of Pre-existing Mitochondria : This was established by using labelled choline in choline-requiring mutant of ***Neurospora crassa.*** Labelled choline is incorporated in mitochondrial lecithin. The cells were examined after a three fold increase in population of mitochondria and each one of them contained labelled choline although they were not previously exposed to labelled choline. The presence of DNA, RNA, protein and phospholipid-synthesizing machinery and indicate metabolic pathways, all indicate their origin from pre-existing organelles. Mechanism involves first growth of the mitochondrial membranes and reproduction of organelles, followed by differentiation and compartmentalization. During the phase of growth membrane area increases, accompanied by elongation of the organelles and then partition by a few cristae forms. Ultimately, a constriction appears which separates the two daughter mitochondria.

(4) Prokaryotic Origin of Mitochondria or Symbiont Hypothesis : The old theory of the bacterial origin of mitochondria has been revived with recent discoveries of similarities in structure and physiology of bacteria and mitochondria.

According to *symbiotic hypothesis,* primitive host cells, which carried out anaerobic respiration by glycolysis, were invaded by bacteria like parasites which respired aerobically through the Kreb's cycle and by oxidative phosphorylation. The invading organisms later developed an endo-symbiotic relationship with the host cells and became the mitochondria. This theory is based on the following several striking similarities between bacteria and mitochondria.

(i) **Morphology :** The general dimensions of bacteria and mitochondria are similar. Rod shaped bacteria are similar in shape to many type of mitochondria.

(ii) **Respiratory Chain :** The inner membrane of mitochondria is similar to the bacterial plasma membrane with respect to the respiratory chain. The projections of plasma membrane (mesosomes) in some bacteria are similar to the cristae of mitochondria.

(iii) **Chemical Composition :** Lipid composition is similar membranes of mitochondria and bacteria. Permease system is similar to that of bacteria.

(iv) **Ribosomes :** The small size of mitochondrial ribosomes. (55-60S) is comparable to that of bacterial ribosomes (70S).

(v) **Drug Sensitivity :** Chloroamphenicol drug inhabits protein synthesis mitochondria and bacteria but not that of higher cells.

(vi) **DNA Structure :** In both case DNA is circular. Circular DNA is found only in prokaryotes. From these similarities one can easily conceive of mitochondria as being evolved from an ancient prokaryote.

6.2 STRUCTURE OF MITOCHONDRIA

A typical mitochondrion is about 15,000 A° long and 5,000 A° in diameter. It is bounded by two membranes, the outer membrane and inner membrane. The space between the two membranes is called *inter-membrane space*. It is about 40-70 A° in width and filled with a watery fluid. The space enclosed by the inner membrane is called *inner-membrane space* or *inner chamber*. This space is filled with a matrix, which contains dense granules, ribosomes and mitochondrial DNA. These granules are considered to be the sites for binding divalent cations partly Mg^{++} and Ca^{++}.

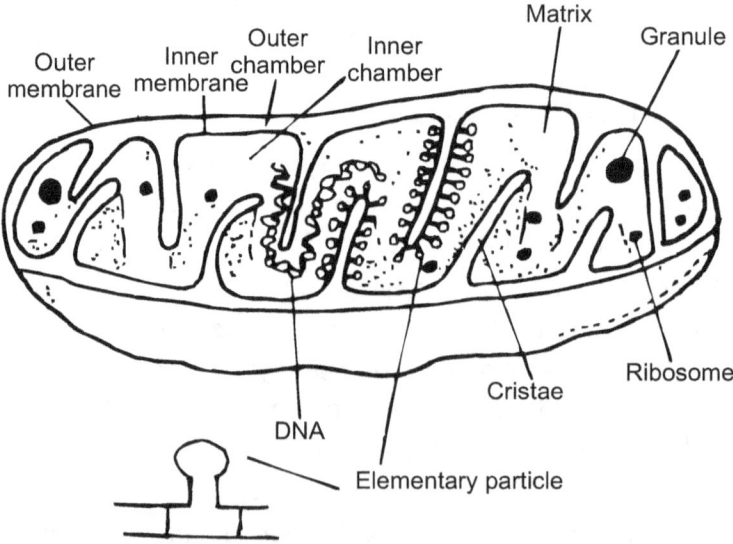

Fig. 6.3 : Mitochondrion; Three Dimensional Diagram, Cut Longitudinally

The inner membrane is thrown up into a series of folds called *mitochondriae cristae*, which projects into the inner chamber. The cavity of the cristae is called the *inter-cristae* space, and is continuous with the intermembrane space.

The outer surface of the outer membrane and the inner surface of inner membrane are supposed to be covered with thousands of small particles. Those on the outer membrane are stackless and are called the *Subunits of Parson*. The particles on the inner membrane are stalked particles and they are called *subunits of Fernandez Moran*. The particles on the inner membrane are considered to be involved in hydrogen transfer.

The outer membrane particles previously were considered to be hollow cylinders, 60 A$^\circ$ long and 60 A$^\circ$ wide with a central hole 20 A$^\circ$ in diameter.

These particles were thought to contain the enzymes of the Krebs cycle. It has however, been shown that enzymes of the Krebs cycle are located in the matrix of mitochondria.

The inner membrane particles consists of base piece, a stalk and a head piece. The particles are spaced about 100 A$^\circ$ intervals. The head piece is 75-100 A$^\circ$ in diameter and the stalk about 50 A$^\circ$ in length. It was formerly thought that each elementary particle contained all the enzymes for electron transport and oxidative phosphorylation. The particles were therefore called Electron Transfer Particles (ETP). Each particle was believed to consist of four complexes with complexes I and II situated in the base piece, complex III in the stalk and complex IV in the head piece.

6.2.1 Chemical Composition

The mitochondrial membrane has a molecular organization, similar to that of plasma membrane. Each membrane is made up of two main substances besides the attached particles. These are proteins and lipids. The proteins are the main constituents and are about 4/5th of the dry weight of the membrane. In its usual form it is insoluble. The lipid forms 1/5th of the weight of the membrane and is found entirely in the form of phospholipids. Each phospholipid molecule is like a clothespin, the head bearing electrically charged atoms and the two legs are formed of long chain fatty acid.

This molecule is insoluble in structural combination which is known as micelle (a group of phospholipid molecules) and becomes soluble. Cholesterol has been found to occur in some, not in all the membranes. Thus, the two membranes of mitochondrion differs in its chemical composition.

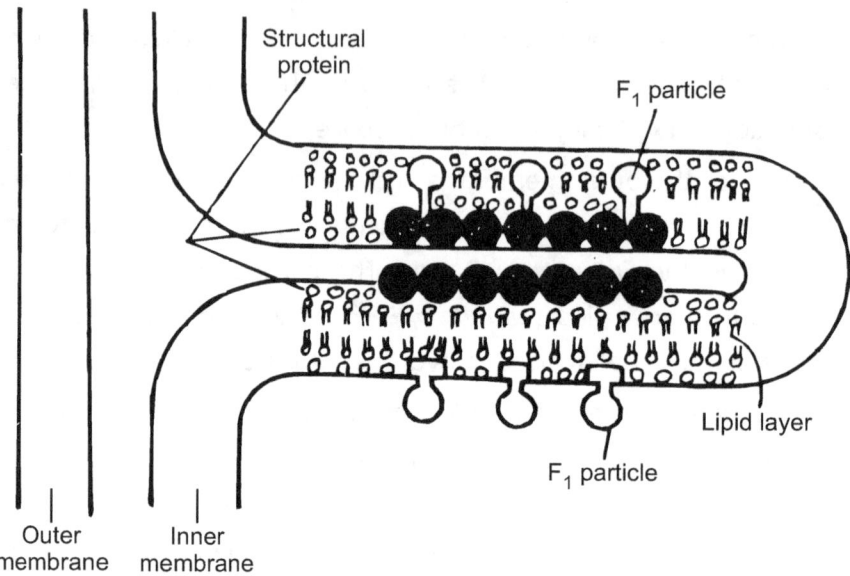

Fig. 6.4 : Mitochondria : Molecular organization of Mitochondrial Crest

6.3 FUNCTIONS OF MITOCHONDRIA

The main mitochondrial function is to generate high energy ATP. Hence, called "the powerhouse of cell. For all the energy consuming processes of the aerobic cells, the energy in the form of ATP is made available by this cell organelle.

As the mitochondria can manufacture the ATP, the molecule having the potential energy is stored as high energy bond. They supply nearly all the required biological energy. Only the mitochondria are fully capable of converting pyruvic acid to carbon dioxide and water.

(1) Cell Respiration : Mitochondria are the respiratory centres of the cell. Cell respiration can be divided into four steps :

(a)   Glycolysis

(b) Oxidation of pyruvic acid

(c)   Krebs/citric acid cycle

(d) Oxidative phosphorylation through hydrogen/electron transport system.

During the cell respiration, good material are oxidized to carbon dioxide and water, in the presence of oxygen. One of the most important fuels is glucose. The overall equation for cell respiraton in the presence of oxygen is :

$$C_6H_{12}O_6 + 6O_2 \rightarrow 6CO_2 + 6 H_2O + Energy$$

Under aerobic condition glucose metabolism takes place in four stages.

(a) Glycolysis : The breakdown of glucose of pyruvic acid is called glycolysis. Glycolysis can take place in the absence of oxygen (anaerobic condition) or in the presence of oxygen (aerobic condition). The enzymes for glycolysis are found in the soluble fraction of the cell, outside the mitochondria.

(b) **Pyruvic Acid Oxidation :** Under aerobic conditions, the pyruvic acid molecule is metabolized to a molecule of acetyl coenzymes A (acetyl CoA).

(c) **Kreb's cycle :** Each acetyl coenzyme A molecule condenses with a molecule of oxaloacetic acid to produce a molecule of citric acid. After several steps, oxaloacetic acid is regenerated. Krebs cycle takes place under aerobic condition. The enzymes for the Kreb's cycle are located in the matrix of the mitochondrion.

(d) **Oxidative Phosphorylation :** It has been seen that pairs of hydrogen (2H) are liberated during aerobic glycolysis, oxidation of pyruvic acid and the Krebs cycle. These hydrogen pairs are passed down the hydrogen/electron transport chain (respiratory chain) and oxidative phosphorylation takes place. Three molecules of ATP are generated per pair of electrons passing down the electron transport chain. The enzymes for electron transport are located in the inner membrane of mitochondrion. The transfer of hydrogens/electrons takes place through a complex chain of hydrogen donors-acceptors consisting of flavoproteins, coenzymes Q and cytochromoes. The respiratory chain is arranged in five complexes (I to V). Oxygen is the final hydrogen acceptor.

(2) **ATP Transport :** The ATP molecules produced as a result of cellular repiration, accumulate in the mitochondria. The mitochondria collect at sites where energy requirement is high. As a result of membrane contraction and increase in internal hydrostatic pressure of the mitochondrion, water and ATP are squeezed out. This results in a lowering of the ATP concentration, and the mitochondrial membrane relaxes. The thyroid hormone thyroxine causes the mitochondria to swell, while ATP brings about contraction.

Points to Remember

- Mitochondria are small granular, filamentous bodies found in the cytoplasm of all aerobic animals and plants.
- The size of mitochondria is also variable.
- The number of mitochondria depends upon the metabolic activity of the cell.
- There are four theories put forth to explain the origin of mitochondria
  a. *De novo* origin of mitochondria.
  b. Mitochondrial formation from other intracellular structures.
  c. Formation by growth and division of pre-exisiting mitochondria.
  d. Prokaryotic origin of mitochondria or symbiont hypothesis.
- The main mitochondrial function is to generate high energy ATP.

Exercise

1. Give an account of the ultrastructure and functions of mitochondria.
2. Explain location, ultrastructure and functions of mitochondria.
3. Mitochondria are the "powerhouse of the cell". Discuss the statement.
4. Describe the structure and function of mitochondria.
5. Discuss the prokaryotic origin of mitochondria.
6. Write short notes on:
    a. Structure of Mitochondria
    b. Morphology of Mitochondria
    c. Chemical composition of Mitochondria
    d. Functions of Mitochondria

Chapter 7

NUCLEUS

- CONTENTS -

7.1 SIZE, SHAPE, NUMBER AND POSITION

(1) Number

Almost all the higher cells possess the nucleus. The mature red blood cells of mammals are without nuclei, however the nuclei are present in the immature stages of the RBCs. Generally, cells usually have a single nucleus called mononucleate cell, but these are different cells which possess more than one nucleus called poly or multinucleate cells. If two nuclei are present called binucleate cell. Examples, ***Parameocium, Vorticella, Balantidium*** exhibits polynucleated cell. The polykaryocytes of bone marrow have upto 100 nuclei. Sometimes some cells do not show cellular boundaries in the mass of protoplasm. Such multinucleate mass of protoplasm is called a ***Syncytium***.

(2) Position

The position of nucleus in a cell is variable. In embryonic cells, the nucleus is central in position but may later become displaced. In adipose tissue cells, nucleus is peripheral, whereas in glandular cells, nucleus is situated at the basal region.

(3) Shape

The shape of the nucleus also varies in different cells. It is generally spherical in cuboidal or polyhedral cells, and disc-shaped in squamous epithelium. In columnar epithelial cells, nucleus is ovoid and elongated. The nuclei are bilobed or multilobed in leukocytes. Other variations in shape, like horse-shoe shaped, branched, pyriform (kidney shaped), spindle shaped, elliptical etc. have also been observed in other cells.

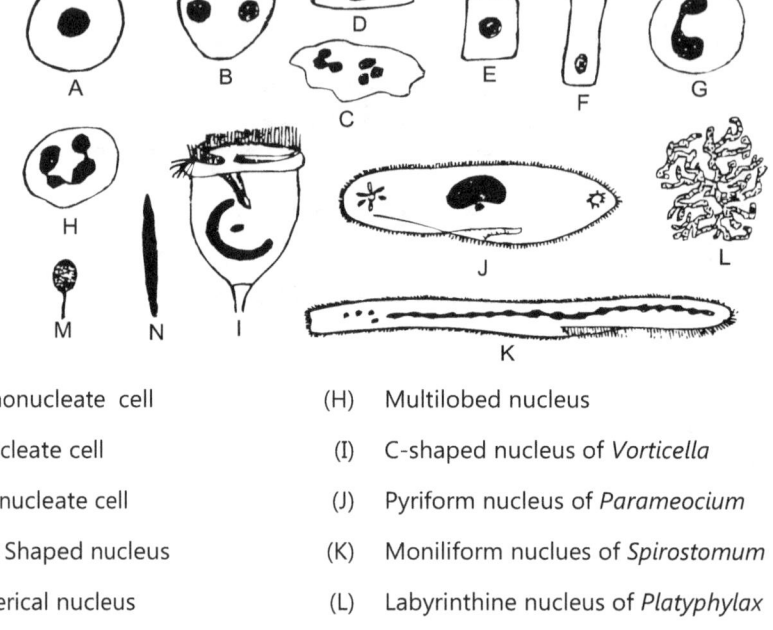

(A)	Mononucleate cell	(H)	Multilobed nucleus
(B)	Binucleate cell	(I)	C-shaped nucleus of *Vorticella*
(C)	Polynucleate cell	(J)	Pyriform nucleus of *Parameocium*
(D)	Disc Shaped nucleus	(K)	Moniliform nuclues of *Spirostomum*
(E)	Spherical nucleus	(L)	Labyrinthine nucleus of *Platyphylax*
(F)	Oval nucleus	(M)	Elliptical nucleus of sperm
(G)	Bilobed nucleus	(N)	Spindle shaped nucleus of sperm.

Fig. 7.1 : Number and Shape of Nuclei

(4) Size

The size of the nucleus also varies according to the cell type. But in general, a ratio exists between the nuclear volume and the volume of the cytoplasm, and this is the characteristic for each cell type. This can be expressed numerically by the nucleoplasmic index. (NP).

$$NP = \frac{\text{Nuclear Volume } (V_n)}{\text{Volume of Cytoplasm } (V_c) - \text{Nuclear Volume } (V_n)}$$

7.2 ULTRASTRUCTURE OF NUCLEAR MEMBRANE AND PORE COMPLEX

The nucleus is bounded by nuclear envelope or membrane or karyotheca. Within the nucleus is a clear or slightly acidophilic mass called the nuclear sap or nuclear matrix. In the interphasic stage the nuclear sap contains twisted filaments of chromatin which are called chromosomes. False nucleoli or karyosomes are nothing but flakes of condensed regions of chromatin are found in the nucleus. One or more spherical bodies called nucleoli or plasmasomes are also observed. Thus, in the nucleus following structures are present.

(1) Nuclear envelope or membrane

(2) Nuclear sap or nuclear matrix

(3) Chromatin

(4) Nucleoli.

7.2.1 Nuclear Envelope

The nucleus is separated from the cytoplasm by a double membrane called the nuclear envelope. The two membranes separated from each other by a perinuclear space of varying width. Each layer is about 100 to 300 A° apart, leaving a discontinuous perinuclear space that communicates with the channels of cytoplasmic membrane. The envelope is absent only during the time of cell division for a very brief period.

Structure of the Envelope

The two membranes of the nuclear envelope are roughly parallel, and each membrane is 70-80 A° thick. Outer membrane has connections with endoplasmic reticulum and has ribosomes on the outer side. The inner membrane possesses a crystalline layer, often coated with filaments and fibrous structures, some of which extend deeper in the nucleus and others may attach to the chromatin material. The nuclear membranes are separated by perinuclear space which is discontinuous except some areas where the membranes join to form pore complex. The two membranes around these pores are in continuity and form a rounded lip around the circular area. The space between the two membranes is irregular, discontinuous and has varying width. The perinuclear space is filled with fluid communicating with the endoplasmic reticulum.

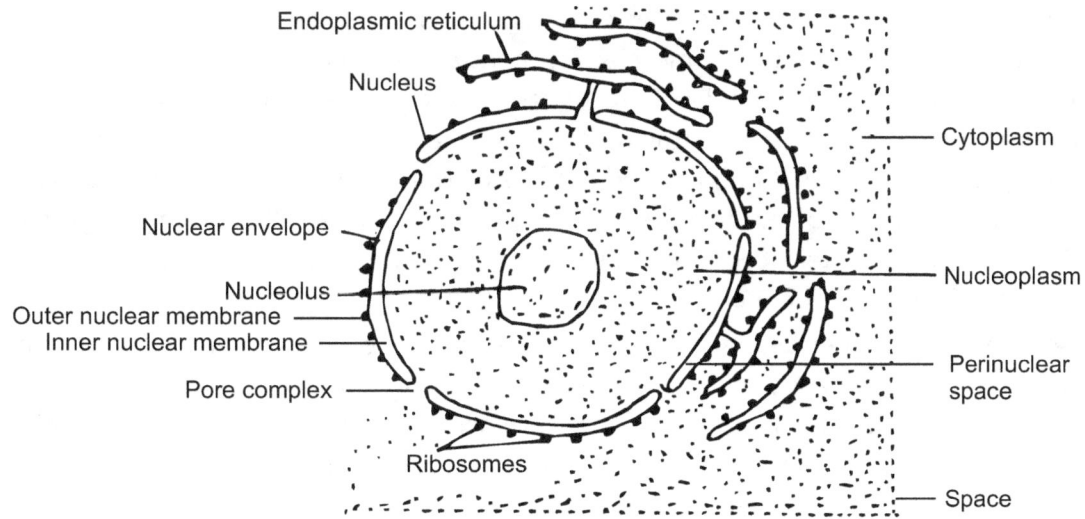

Fig. 7.2 : Nucleus with Nuclear Envelope and Nuclear Pores

7.2.2 Pore Complex

The nuclear envelope is interrupted at intervals by nuclear pores which act as passage ways for transport of various types of materials. In plant cells these pores are irregularly and sparsely distributed over the surface of the nucleus, but in certain animal cells (e.g. amphibian oocyte) the pores are numerous and regularly arranged. It has been observed that the number of pores per unit area of the envelope varies with cell types and with the physiological state of the cell. The pores are aligned with the nucleoplasmic channels. The number of pores range from 100 to 5×10^7 in different cells. It seems that the pore number is related to pore density and the number of RNA molecules being transported from the nucleus.

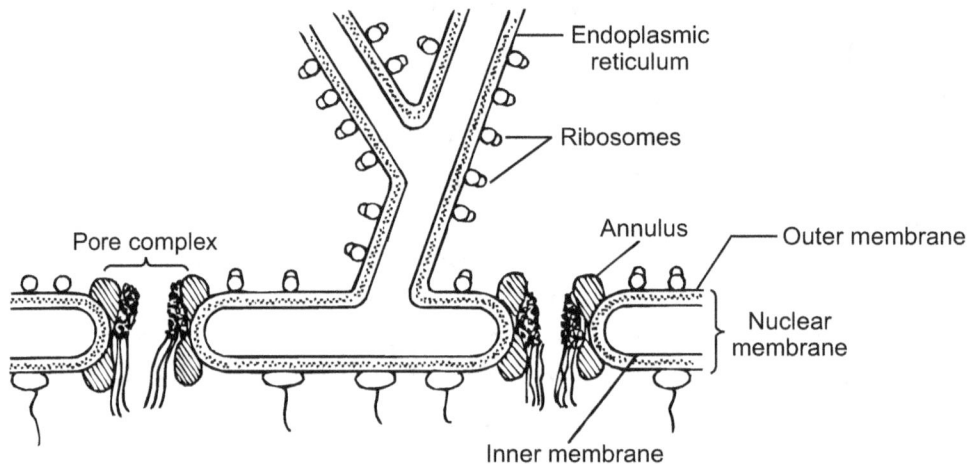

Fig. 7.3 : Nuclear Envelope and its Relationship with Endoplasmic Reticulum

The pores are also arranged in rows or hexagonal clusters, electron microscopic studies showed that the pores contain some electron-dense materials and are enclosed by some annular material, which is granular. Pore diameter also varies from cell to cell, generally from 50 to 100 nm. These circular structures are called annuli, which along with pores form a pore complex. The annulus is ring like and consists of eight granules, each with a diameter of 15 – 17 nm. The matrix of the annulus may be amorphous or fibrillar which is digested by trypsin and hence is proteinaceous in nature. It is however, not hydrolysed by nucleases. The pore complex is a rigid structure.

Below the inner membrane of nuclear envelope there is an internal dense lamella, composed of homogeneous material called the honey comb layer, which is bordered by lumps of chromatin on the inner surface. The thickness of lamella varies from 200 to 800 A°. The nuclear envelope shows connections with the nuclear components as well as the cytoplasmic region. The dense chromatin region or layer is interrupted below the pores giving rise to intranuclear channels, which open on the nuclear surface through the pores.

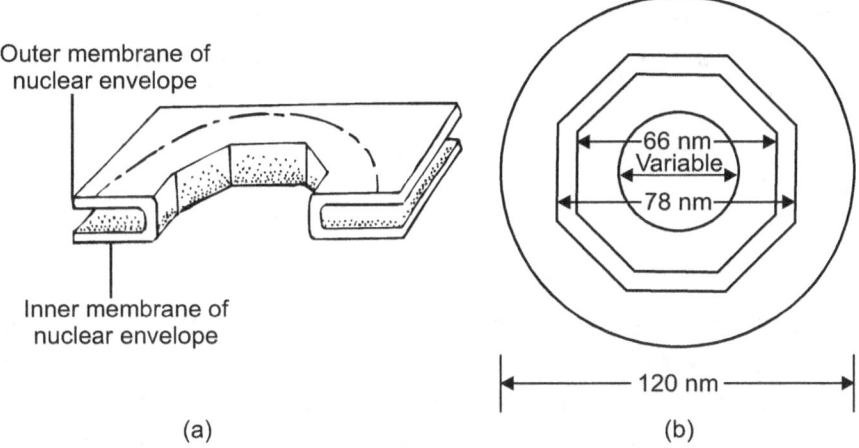

Fig. 7.4 (A) : Structure of Nuclear Pore, Diameter of Nuclear Pore

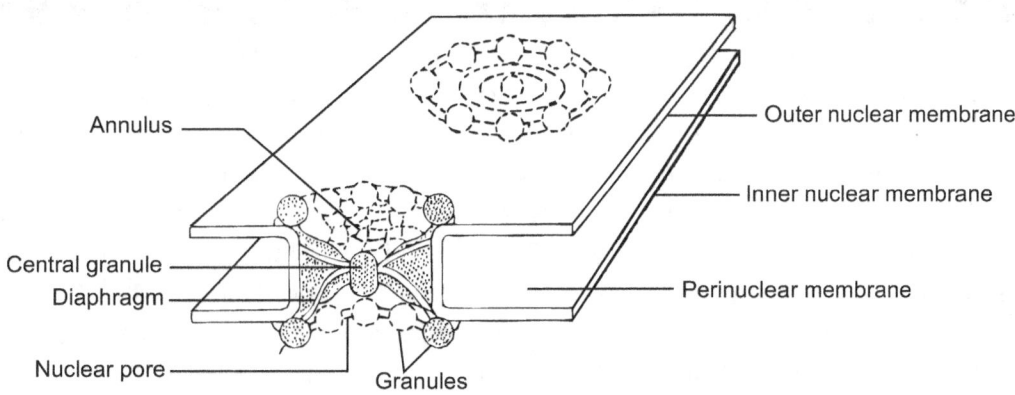

Fig. 7.4 (B) : Nuclear Pore Complex in the Nuclear Membrane

7.3 NUCLEAR SAP/NUCLEAR MATRIX

The body of the nucleus within the nuclear envelope is made up of a dense jelly-like mass which is composed of two elements, each of which is dynamic in nature and has complex chemical composition. These elements of nuclear sap are the nuclear gel or karyolymph and the chromatin.

The Nuclear Gel : It is highly granular, containing fibrous material. It is rich in proteins, which account for more than 90% the material. A small percentage of DNA, RNA and Phospholipids is also present. The proteins are largely acidic and they have an unusual property of expanding and contracting under the influence of Ca^{2+} and Mg^{2+} ions. In this region, events like replication of DNA, transcription and transport of substances take place.

The Chromatin : The other components of the nuclear matrix include nucleolus and chromatin. The chromatin is present in a condensed form called heterochromatin, which is present in patches near the nuclear envelope, either scattered in the interior or surrounding the nucleoli. The matrix also has a network of non-chromatin material forming interchromatin matrix.

Functions : The nuclear matrix plays three important functions such as :

(i)   DNA replication

(ii) DNA transcription

(iii) Post transcriptional processing.

It was first thought that the site of DNA replication lies in the vicinity of nuclear envelope. This assumption was based on the observation that the most of the chromatin material is localised on the nuclear side of the envelope. However, latest findings suspended in the matrix. Matrix is made up of some proteins which can be easily digested or hydrolysed by enzyme pepsin.

7.4 NUCLEOLUS

The nucleolus was first recognized by Fontona in 1874. It is generally spherical shaped body situated in the nucleus either in a central or peripheral region. The number of nucleoli in each nucleus depends on the species or the sets of chromosomes present in the nucleus. The number of nucleoli in each nucleus may be 1, 2, or 4. Nucleolus is the characteristic feature of eukaryotic cells, while it is absent in prokaryotic cells. The size of nucleolus depends on the synthetic activity of the cell. Thus, the cells with little or no synthetic activities e.g. sperm cells, muscle cells, are found to contain smaller or no nucleoli, while the oocytes, neurons and secretary cells which synthesize the proteins or other substances contain large sized nucleoli. The size varies from 1 to 5 μm in diameter.

General Organisation

Under light microscope, the nucleolus appears as a fluid or semisolid homogeneous body. It shows four main components namely granules, fibrils, matrix and chromatin.

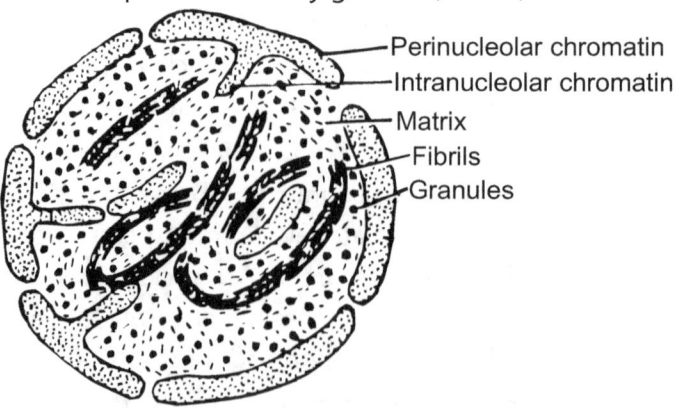

Fig. 7.5 : Nucleolus

(i) **Granules :** The granular region generally occurs densely at the periphery of the nucleolus. These granules are of 150 to 200 A° in diameter. The granules contain ribo-nucleoproteins in which RNA and proteins are in ratio of 1 : 2. These granules are generally modify into ribosomes. All the granules are connected together by a thin filament resembling a string with beads.

(ii) **Fibrils :** Fibrillar region is also known as ***nucleolonema***. It is mainly composed by many fine fibres called fibrils. They are made up of ribonucleic proteins and with 50 – 80 A° in length. Both granules and fibrils are digested by ribonuclease enzyme.

(iii) **Matrix :** This is also called amorphous or proteinous region. The granules and fibrils are point out that nuclear matrix is the major site whose DNA replication first takes place and later it gets associated with the nuclear envelope also.

Nuclear matrix is also the site of transcription because a certain amount of residual RNA is found associated with the matrix protein. Subsequently, RNA undergoes post transcriptional changes in the matrix itself where it is possessed to smaller RNA pieces, which ultimately pass through the nuclear pores into the cytosol.

Nucleolus also contains electron dense chromatin material, usually at the periphery. Chromatin is composed of fibres of 100 A° thickness. The chromatin contains DNA, which serves are template for RNA synthesis. Surrounding the nucleolus like a shell is perinucleolar chromatin. Projecting into the nucleolus from the perinucleolar chromatin are septa like trabeculae which constitute intranucleolar chromatin.

Chemical Composition

As far as the chemical composition of nucelolus is concerned 5 to 10% of the nucleolus is made up of RNA and remaining part is made-up of protein. The main protein components are phosphoproteins. Acid phosphatase, nucleoside phosphorylase and NAD^+ synthesizing enzymes have been localised in the nucleolus. It is surrounded by a ring of Feulgen positive chromain which actually represents the heterochromatin regions of chromosomes.

Functions of Nucleolus

(1) **Ribosome Formation :** Nucleolus is involved in the biogenesis of ribosomes.

(2) **RNA Production :** Nucleolus is one of the most active sites of RNA synthesis. It produces about 70-90% of cellular RNA in many cells. It is also the source of ribosomal RNA (rRNA).

(3) **Protein Synthesis :** Maggio (1960) and others have suggested that the protein synthesis takes place in the nucleolus. Some cell biologists suggested that ribosomal proteins are synthesized by nucleolus.

(4) **Role in Mitosis :** The nucleolus plays a significant role in mitosis.

7.5 NUCLEOCYTOPLASMIC INTERACTIONS

Most of the nucelic acids like DNA and RNA of cell are formed in the nucleus and those found in the cytoplasm are thought to have migrated there. The main exceptions are related to the DNA of some cytoplasmic organelles. Messenger RNA is formed in the nucleus, in association with the chromosomes. Ribosomal RNA is also formed in the nucleus, especially in the nucleolus. Since, some protein synthesis goes on in the nucleus m-RNA and ribosomes first become associated with the nucleus, to form functional polysomes. Most polysomes are found in the cytoplasm and it is assumed that they migrate these through the pores in the nuclear membrane. Recently, evidence has been obtained for the existence of a particle which appears in the nucleus but rapidly becomes associated with polysomes in the cytoplasm. This particles contain a precursor of the 40S ribosomal sub-particle and possibly mRNA. It may associate with 60S sub-particle forming molecule of mRNA. Other ribosomes may then become attached and may be extensively reused in the cytoplasm.

Some polysomes remain free in the cell sap but become bound to the membranes of the ER.

Cytoplasmic nucelic acids are synthesized in the nucleus. RNA might act as a template for a synthesis of more RNA in the cytoplasm. The cytoplasm might have DNA containing structures. Cytoplasmic DNA falls into three categories. In some amphibian eggs large amount of DNA in cytoplasm is present. It may have function in regulating the early development of embryo. The cells of microorganisms and protozoa have self replicating DNA containing particles called episomes. They exist free in the cytoplasm or in intimate association with the chromosome.

Cellular activity is controlled by the nucleus and more specifically by DNA located in the chromosomes. The RNA involves in protein synthesis originates in the nucleus and is then transferred to the cytoplasm. It is generally accepted that some macromolecules, small organic molecules, water and ions can pass across the nuclear envelope. These macromolecules can cross the nuclear envelope through nuclear pores, by active transport by blebbing and exchange through the endoplasmic reticulum. Many studies suggest that granular material of nucelolar origin pass from the nucleus to the cytoplasm, and may be involved in the biogenesis of ribosomes.

Points to Remember

- Cells that have a single nucleus are called mononucleate cells while those that possess more than one nucleus are called poly or multinucleate cells.

- The nucleoplasmic index - a ratio of the nuclear volume and the volume of the cytoplasm is characteristic for each cell type.

- The nucleus is separated from the cytoplasm by a double membrane called the nuclear envelope.

- The two membranes of the nuclear envelope – outer and inner are roughly parallel.

- The nuclear pores present in the nuclear envelope are passage ways for transport of various types of materials.

- The nuclear gel and the chromatin are the elements of nuclear sap.

- Nucleolus is a fluid or semisolid homogeneous body having four main components - granules, fibrils, matrix and chromatin.

- Almost all the higher cells possesses the nucleus. Their size, shape, number and position also variable.

- The nucleus is bounded by nuclear envelope or membrane or karyotheca. It is having following structure :
  a. Nuclear envelope or membrane
  b. Nuclear sap or nuclear matrix
  c. Chromatin
  d. Nucleoli

- The body of nucleus within the nuclear envelope is made op of dense-like mass and has complex chemical composition.

- Cellular activity is controlled by the nucleus and more specifically by DNA located in the chromosomes.

Exercise

1. Describe the structure of interphase nucleus.

2. Discuss the structure and functions of nucleus.

3. Name the various components of nucleus. Give an account of the structure and functions of each.

4. Describe morphology of nucleus and functions of nuclear envelope.

5. Describe the morphology, position and size of nucleus and add a note on functions of nucleus.

6. Write short notes on:

    a. Nuclear envelope

    b. Functions of nucleus

    c. Nuclear matrix

    d. Nuclear cytoplasmic interactions

    e. Functions of nuclear envelope

    f. Pore complex

    g. Nucleolus

    h. Nucleoprotein

CYTOSKELETON

- CONTENTS -

8.1 MICROTUBULES

The cytoplasm of the most eukaryotic cells contain two types of very slender, fine proteinaceous thread-like structures called *microtubules* and *microfilaments*. These are useful for performance of two major cellular functions namely production of cell shape and motility. They are absent in prokaryotes.

Microtubules are hollow fibrillar structures which were first of all observed in the axoplasm of the myelinated nerves fibres by **De Robertis** and **Franchi** (1953). They called them neurotubules. The exact nature of microtubules was studied by **Sabatini** and **Barnett** (1963) using glutaraldehyde fixative in electron microscopy.

8.1.1 Occurrence

The microtubules occur in cytoplasm giving structural support to the cells hence they are also called cytoskeleton. These structures occur either in the form of bundles or sheets. The bundles may consists of a few as two or three to several hundred microtubules. They are essentially rigid structures but they can also bend and form arches.

Microtubules are found in the cytoplasm of both animal and plant cells at seven various sites :

(1) **Cilia and Flagella :** The cilicum or flagellum contains 11 longitudinal fibrils, 2 central and 9 peripheral. The central 2 microtubules are similar in structure to cytoplasmic microtubules. Each microtubule is hollow cylinder composed of 13 longitudinal protofilaments. The 9 peripheral fibrils are doublet microtubules appearing like a figure of 8 in transverse section.

(2) **Centrioles and Basal Bodies :** The wall of each centrioles consists of 9 peripheral fibrils. Each fibril is made up of 3 subfibres or microtubules called A, B and C. A subfibre is complete and tubular whereas B and C are incomplete.

(3) **Microtubules in Nerve Cells :** They are present along the length of the axons of nerve cells called nerotubules. They consists of 13 parallel filaments with 50 A° diameter. They are formed by tubulin. They are useful for structural support and fast transport of substances down to axon.

(4) **Microtubules in Axopodia of Protozoa :** They are located in axopodia of protozoa and in sperm tail.

(5) **Microtubules in Thrombocytes :** The human and rat thrombocytes or platelets show 8-24 microtubules very close to cell membrane.

(6) **Microtubules in the Mitotic Spindle :** There are spindle fibres of microtubules in mitotic spindle. Their number varies from 16 (in yeast cells) to over 5000 in higher plant cells.

(7) **Microtubules in Sensory Cells :** The sensory cells in inner ear, rods and cone cells of retina and ocelli show cilia like structures. These cilia have a peripheral doublet in which mircotubules are present. The central two tubules are short or absent. In case of insects, the sensory cells show bundles of microtubules of 300 to 700.

8.1.2 Structure

The microtubules are long, hollow cylinders with 210 to 250 A° diameter and several microns in length. The wall thickness is about 50 A° and the hollow core of about 150 A°. The microtubule contains 13 subunits or protofilaments which lie parallel to the long axis.

The protofilament is made up of a linear series of globular protein called tubulin units arranged. like a string of beads. The size of each unit is 50 A° ×40 A°. Actually, tubulin is a dimer composed of two similar, but not identical, polypeptides. The subunits are called α-tubulin and β-tubulin with molecular weights of 55,000 and 57,000 respectively. The amino acid composition of two subunits are similar. The α and β tubulin units are arranged alternately in the profilament. Tubulin units are arranged in a helical manager with β tubulin molecules per turn of helix.

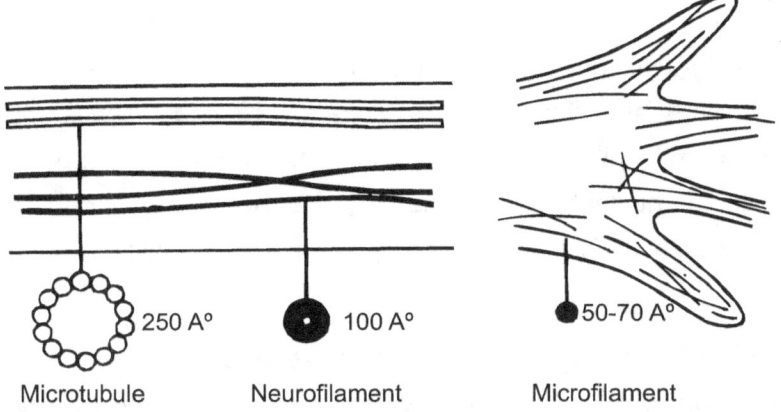

Fig. 8.1 : Different Types of Fibrillar Structures in Nerve Cells

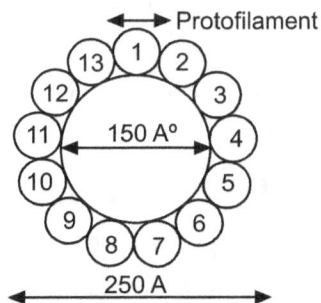

(B) Transverse of microtueuie showing the 13 protofilaments forming the wall of the tubule

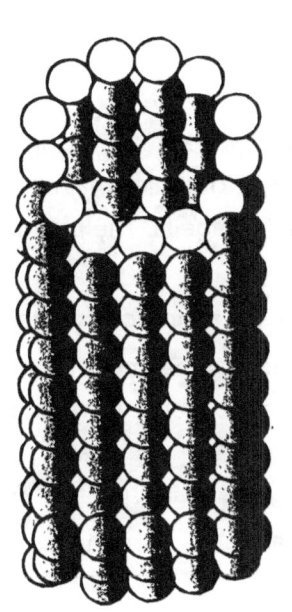

(A) Three-dimensional model of microtubule structure

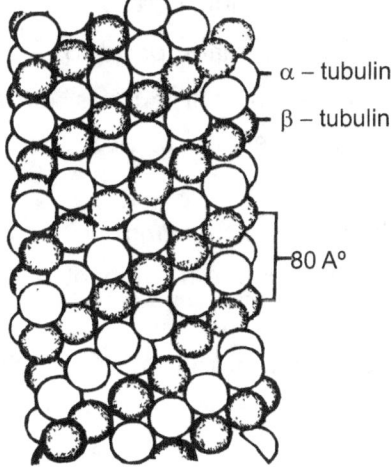

(C) Surface view of microtubule showing probable arrangements of units. Each monomer is roughly spherical (50 A° × 40 A°).

Fig. 8.2 : Structure of Microtubule

In addition to the tubulins there are also 20 to 25 secondary proteins called Microtubule Associated Proteins (MAPs). They are useful for function of microtubules and in the control of assembly. The tubulines at different sites (cilia and brain) are similar but not identical. Flagellar and cytoplasmic tubulins are also different. The flagellar and brain tubulins are associated with Gaunine nucleotide. Each tubulin dimer has two nucleotide binding sites and is bound to two molecules of GTP. One molecule is bound strongly and other weakly.

8.1.3 Microtubule Assembly

The microtubule of cilia, flagella and axostyle are stable and under normal conditions they do not breakdown and reassemble. However, the microtubules of cytoplasm are labile and they readily undergo reversible assembly and disassembly. The poison *colchicin* which inhibits microtubule assembly because it binds tightly to subunit proteins and preventing their polymerization. In dividing cells mitosis is blocked at metaphase because of breakdown of the spindle microtubules, leading to *polyploidy*. Therefore, colchicine is used to produce polyploid varieties of plants.

8.1.4 Functions of Microtubules

Microtubules perform the following important functions of cells :

(1) The microtubules are somewhat rigid and form the supporting network in the cytoplasm. Thus, they form cytoskeleton and give the shape to the cell. Microtubules maintain the shape of axons of nerve cells, axopodia of protozoans, cilia and flagella. The biconcave shape of RBCs is maintained by microtubules.

(2) Microtubules give axial support to cilia, flagella and thus, helps in their movements.

(3) Microtubules act as cell muscles and are involved in cell membrane movements at the time of projection of pseudopodia, endocytosis, projection and retraction of microvilli.

(4) Microtubules form the mitotic apparatus or spindle during cell division. Their contraction causes the movement of the chromosomes towards the opposite poles of the cells.

(5) Microtubules and microfilaments which occur in axon of nerve cells are useful for the transport of proteins and other substances synthesized in cell body down to axon. The microtubules form microcirculatory system for intracellular transport of water and inorganic ions. In melanocytes pigment granules are transported by microtubules. They are also involved in release of insulin from P-cells of pancreas.

(6) The microtubules are also involved in change of shape of cell. During cell differentiation cells change their shape and microtubules plays an important role in the process of differentiation.

(7) Microtubules also act a transducer, converting stimuli into nerve impulses.

In cells, there are variety of different types of fibrillar or filamentous structures which are seen only under electron microscope. The filaments are of two types namely microfilaments and the larger neurofilamens found in the axons of nerve cells.

8.2 MICROFILAMENTS

The microfilaments are specific type of fibrous elements having diameter of 50 to 70 A° and they are composed of protein actin which is usually found in muscle. The microfilaments are found in clusters beneath the cell membrane. A microfilament is a single strand of identical globular protein having a molecular weight about 4200 daltons.

Actin when present in monomeric form is called G-actin. Globular actin (G-actin) is capable of assembling *in-vivo* or *in-vitro* into a double stranded filament called F-actin or fibrous actin. Actin filaments are capable of interacting with another protein called myosin and with myosin it forms actomyosin.

Observations made on wide variety of cells have indicated that microfilaments form. The major components of contractile machinery of the cell. In addition to their role in muscle contraction, microfilaments also help in cytokinesis, cell movement, nerve outgrowth, tubular gland formation, movement of the inersititial microvilli, cytoplasmic streaming and gastrulation. They are not only playing mechanical function but they could store energy by distortion and during disassembly they could release elastic forces that might transport cytoplasmic structures.

Microfilaments are arranged in to different ways. In one arrangement they arranged in parallel bundles near the surface of cell membrane. These bundles also contain other muscle proteins like myosin, tropomyosin and α-actinin in cultured cells like chicken fibroblasts. The another type of arrangement of microfilamens is in the form of a loose meshwork. Which is seen in the pseudopodia of *Amoeba*. Indirect evidence indicates that microfilaments are involved in movement associated with furrow formation in cell division, cytoplasmic streaming in plant cells, amoeboid motion in amoebae, leucocytes, culture cells and cell migration during embryonic development.

8.3 NEUROFILAMENTS

The microfilaments present in the nerve cells are called neurofilaments which are longer filaments. The neurofilaments have a diameter of about 100 A° and travel along the length of most axons. They appear tetragonal with unstained central canal in transverse section under electron microscope. The protein component of neurofilament has molecular weight of 70,000. It is not tubulin or actin protein. The function of neurofilaments is in the transport of material from their site of synthesis in the cyton to the end of the axon. There are two types of transport mechanisms observed, slow transport involving soluble and particulate components and fast transport carrying organellies and particles.

List of the Proteins Associated with Microfilaments

(1) Actin

(2) Myosin, Minimyosin

(3) Tropomyosin

(4) Tropomin – C

(5) α-actin

(6) Actin Binding and cross linking proteins

   (i) Fimbrin, (ii) Spectrin, (iii) α-actinin, (iv) Filamin.

(7) Actin severing and capping proteins.

   (i) Villin, (ii) Gelsolin, (iii) Acumetin.

(8) Actin-Depolymerizing proteins.

   (i) Profilin

8.3.1 Helical Structure of F-actin

Microfilament are composed of contractile proteins i.e. actin and myosin. Besides these two tropomyosin, tropomin –C, α - actin and other proteins found in muscles are also found in microfilament. Actin filaments are made up of globular actin molecule (G-actin) arranged end to end to produce F-actin. The non-muscle cell also contain actin and myosin contractile proteins. The contraction or relaxation in these cells is also similar to that of muscle and the force generated by sliding mechanism.

In the case of non-muscle cells, however cycles of polymerization and depolymerization of actin may play a prominent role in cell movement.

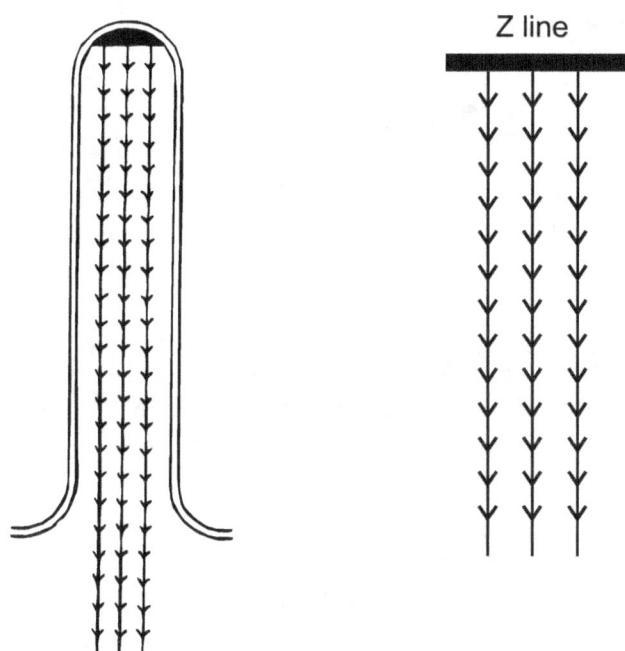

Fig. 8.3 : Polarity of the Actin Filaments in Microvillus and Skeletal Muscles

In non-muscle cells actin may appear in a variety of structural forms. For example, in intestinal microvilli, actin microfilaments are well ordered and have regular polarization. The stress fibres, observed in spreading moving cells in culture are also formed by bundles of actin microfilaments.

These structures also contain other proteins such as myosin, tropomyosin, α-actinin and filamin. In other parts of cells e.g. in pseudopodia, ruffling membranes, and in the bulk of cytoplasm actin filaments are disposed at random and form a cross linked network. It is currently believed that the changes in viscosity of the cytoplasm are due to rapid modifications in the actin network.

Actin comprises a large proportion of the cytoplasmic proteins of many cells in developing nerve cells. It may constitute upto 20% of these proteins. Actin is present principally in it, in globular form (G-actin) with a molecular weight of 42,000 daltons and it may quickly polymerize to form the microfilaments of fibrous actin (F-actin) which may measure several micrometres in length and contain thousands of monomers.

Cytoplasmic actin is very similar in structure to muscle actin and forms identical 6 nm wide microfilaments consisting of a double helical array of globular actin molecules. The actin meromyosin complex has an arrow-like shape with a definite polarity. By comparison with an arrow it is possible to recognize a 'pointed' and a 'barbed' end.

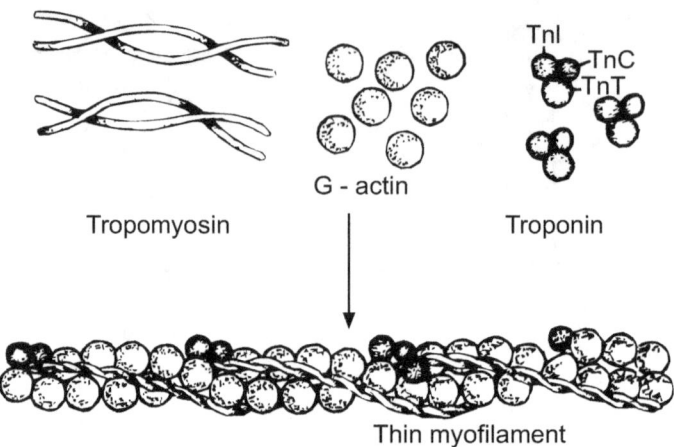

Fig. 8.4 : F-actin

Although actin monomers can be added to both ends. The barbed one is preferred for assembly, while at the pointed end deassembly takes place. This type of polarization is somewhat similar to that observed in microtubules and in both cases the process is often called tread milling. Actin filaments result from the aggregation of a few monomers of G-actin by the process called nucleation. At these nucleation centres more monomers are added to the ends. Actin filaments can fragments spontaneously to produce new nucleation.

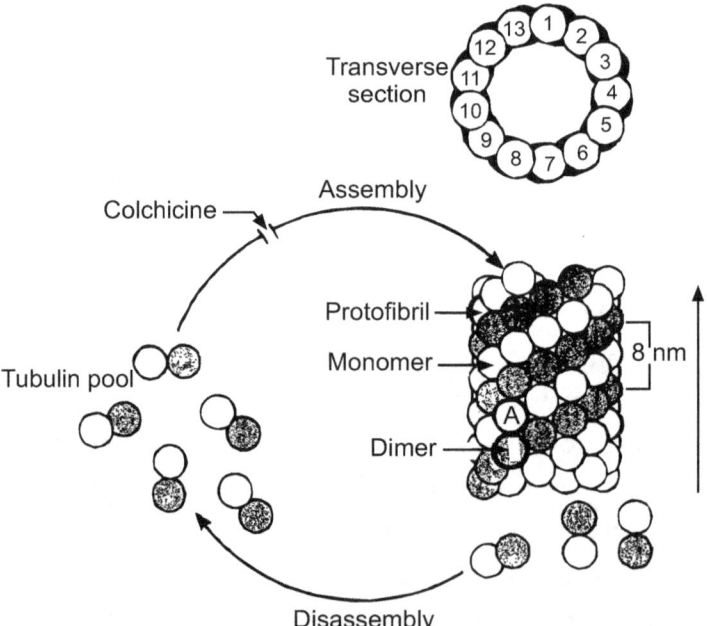

Fig. 8.5 : Process of Assembly and Disassembly of Tubulin which somewhat similar in F-actin

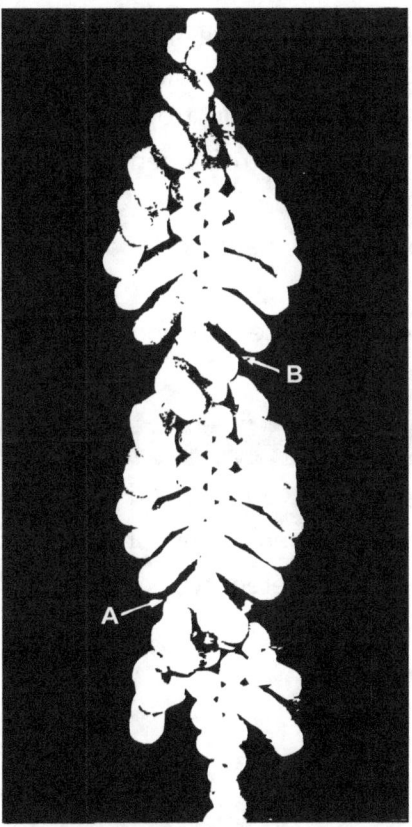

Fig. 8.6 : Helical Structure of G-actin and F-actin

Points to Remember

- The cytoplasm of most eukaryotic cell contain two types of very slender, fine proteinaceous thread like structures called microtubules and microfilaments.

- Microtubules are found in the cytoplasm of both animal and plant cells at seven various sites like Cilia and flagella, centrioles and basal bodies, microtubules in nerve cells, microtubules in axopodia of protozoa and microtubules in thrombocytes, microtubules in the mitotic spindle, microtubules in sensory cells.

- The microtubules are long, hollow cylinder with 210 to 250 A° diameter and contain 13 subunits and made up of globular protein called tubulin.

- Microtubules give axial support to cilia, flagella and thus in their movements.

- It is also acts a Transducer, converting stimuli into nerve impulses as well as involved in changing the shape of cells.

- The microfilaments are specific type of fibrous elements having diameter of 50 to 70 A°, composed of actin protein.

- Actin present in monomeric form called G-actin or globular actin.
- Microfilaments are arranged in parallel bundles near the surface of cell membrane and contain another muscle protein like myosin, tropomyosin.
- Another types of arrangements of microfilaments is in the form of a loose meshwork, found in pseudopodia of *Amoeba*.
- The microfilaments present in the nerve cells are neurofilaments, which are longer filaments.
- The function of neurofilaments is in the transport of material from their sites of synthesis in the cyton to the end of the axon.

Exercise

1. What is Microtubule? Describe its occurrence and structure of microtubule.
2. Describe the structure and arrangement of microtubule. Add note on functions.
3. What is Microfilament ? Describe different types of microfilaments.
4. Write short notes on :
   (a) Helical structure of F-actin.
   (b) Neurofilaments
   (c) Functions of microfilaments
5. Differentiate between Microtubules and Microfilaments.

Chapter 9

CELL CYCLE AND CELL DIVISION

- CONTENTS -

9.1 MITOSIS

All organisms that reproduce sexually develop from a single cell, the zygote, produced by the union of two cells, the germ cells or gametes. Development from zygote to the full grown stage takes place by the division of cells. Even after development in the body of the organism, replacement of cells takes place by cell division. In the multicellular animals, two types of cells are present, namely *somatic cells* and *germ cells*. The somatic cells are responsible for the formation of different parts of the body and germ cells form the gametes : sperms and ova. Mitosis or somatic cell division is the multiplication of the somatic cells into daughter cells of equal size both containing the same number of chromosomes as the parent cell. The term mitosis (Greek; *mitos* - thread) refers to the threadlike appearance of chromosomes in the early cell division. At the time of mitosis nucleus becomes completely reorganised. The mitotic cycle is divided into series of consecutive phases known as prophase, metaphase, anaphase and telophase. The period between two mitotic cycles is called interphase.

Mitosis involves a series of complex changes in both the nucleus and cytoplasm. The division of nucleus is called karyokinesis and the division of cytoplasm called *cytokinesis*.

Interphase : This is the so called 'resting phase' but it is a period of intense biosynthetic activity. Cells however, spend most of their life-span in interphase. Three important processes which are preparatory to cell division, take place during interphase.

1. Replication of DNA takes place and also synthesis of basic nuclear proteins, the histones.

2. The centrioles divide, forming a pair of new centrioles which are right angles to each other.

3. During interphase, energy rich compounds are synthesized and they provide energy for mitosis. The proteins which are found in the spindle, are also synthesized at the end of interphase.

Interphase is further divided into three phases, G_1, S and G_2.

1. G_1 phase : It is also called post mitotic gap phase (G_1) which takes place at the end of cell division. In this phase, there is no DNA synthesis, however, RNA and proteins are synthesized.

2. S phase : This is called synthesis phase in which DNA is synthesized and is doubled.

3. G_2 phase : This is pre-mitotic gap phase in which synthesis of RNA and protein continues but DNA synthesis stops. It is the interval between end of DNA synthesis and start of mitosis. The cells which do not divide frequently have a longer G_1 phase, while frequently dividing cells have a shorter phase. Various stimuli can terminate G_1, phase, and cell division then starts. As the cell enters the S-phase, it synthesizes DNA and usually commits itself to division. During interphase chromosomes are duplicated.

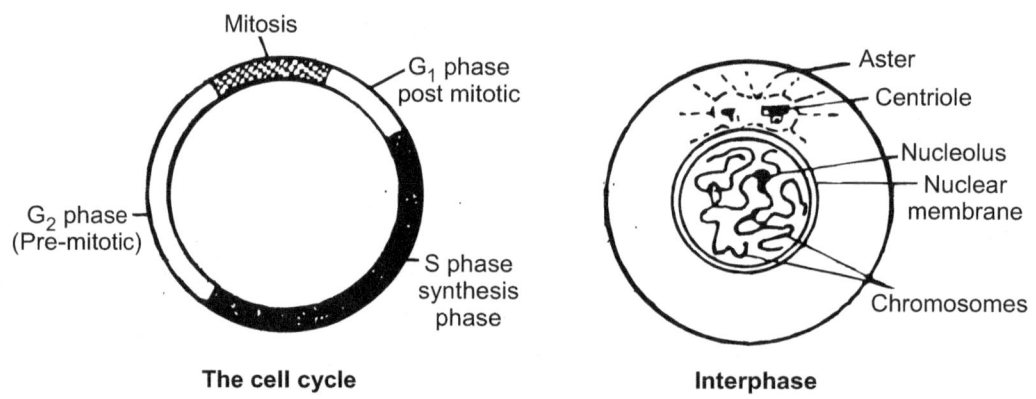

The cell cycle   Interphase

Fig. 9.1 : Cell Cycle and Interphase

(1) Prophase : It is the longest stage of mitosis and lasts from one to several hours. During prophase, the cell becomes spherical and there is increase in viscosity and refractivity. The nucleus shows enlargement due to intake of water. The chromosomes start to condense by a process of folding of the chromatin fibres. Prophase chromosome is composed of two coiled chromatids which are a result of the replication of DNA during S phase. Chromatids are united by a centromere and is called dyad. As prophase progresses, the chromatids become shorter and thicker and chromosomes are evenly distributed in the nuclear cavity.

They migrate towards the nuclear envelope, leaving central clear empty space. At this time, each chromosome is composed of two cylindrical, parallel elements and they show primary and secondary constrictions. Other changes are the reduction in size of the nucleoli, and their disintegration within the nucleoplasm. At the end of prophase, the nuclear envelope is rapidly fragmented and disappears releasing nuclear material into the cytoplasm.

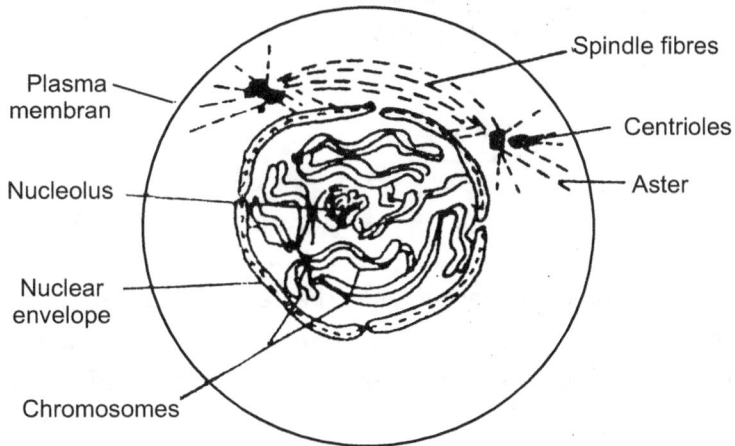

Fig. 9.2 : Prophase

The most conspicuous change which occurs in the cytoplasm is the spindle formation. In the early prophase, there are two pairs of centrioles, each one surrounded by the aster, composed of microtubules that radiate in all directions. The asters are cytoplasmic in origin. The two pairs of centrioles migrate towards opposite poles of the cell. They are pushed apart by the growth of the spindle fibres between them.

Pro-metaphase : Sometimes transition between prophase and metaphase is called pro-metaphase. This is a short period in which the nuclear envelope disintegrates and the chromosomes are in apparent disorder. There is no differentiation between cytoplasm and nuceloplasm. Such mitosis is called extranuclear mitosis or eumitosis.

In some protozoa and animal cells, the nuclear membrane remains intact and mitosis takes place within the nuclear membrane called intranuclear mitosis or premitosis. The chromosomes move freely through this area as they need towards the equator.

(2) Metaphase : In this stage, the chromosomes reach the central or equatorial portion of the spindle. They become radially oriented in the equatorial plate to form the equatorial plate. Those fibres of the spindle that connect to the chromosomes are generally called the chromosomal fibres, those that extend without interruption from one pole to the other are called continuous fibres. The centriloes lie on the equator of the spindle. Usually, the arms of the chromosomes lie on the equator of spindle. Occasionally, only the centromeres lie on the equatorial plane and arms are directed towards the poles.

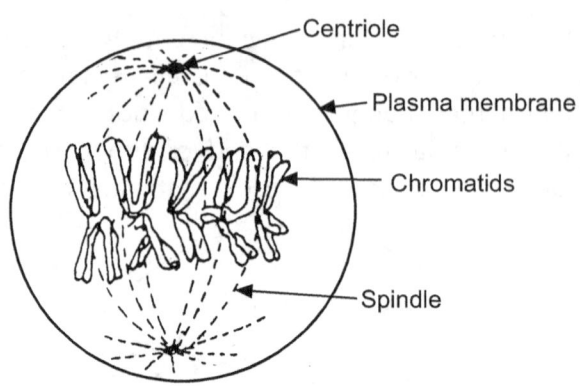

Fig. 9.3 : Metaphase

Mitosis in which the spindle has centrioles and asters is called *astral or amphiastral* and is found in animal cells and some lower plants. Mitosis in which centrioles and asters are absent, is called *anastral* and is found in higher plants. Thus, centrioles and asters are not indispensable to the formation of the spindle, and in a certain way, the formation of spindle in astral mitosis is a mechanism that leads to the distribution of the centrioles between the two daughter cells. Spindles are of two types, *direct* and *indirect*. In the direct type, chromosomal fibres connect the chromosomes directly with the pole and in the indirect type, the chromosomes are connected with continuous fibres.

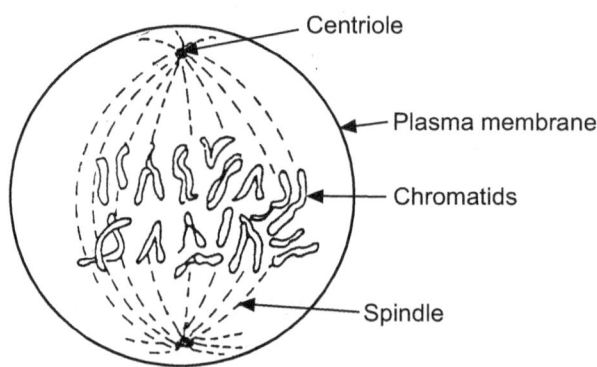

Fig. 9.4 : Early Anaphase

(3) Anaphase : The centromeres of the chromosomes, arranged on equatorial plate, divide simultaneously as anaphase commences, and the two chromatids of each pair separate. They are now called *daughter chromosomes*. The centromeres move apart and the chromatids also start moving towards the poles. The forces behind chromosome movement are not yet known.

Fig. 9.5 : Late Anaphase

It is suggested that the chromosomes are pulled by chromosomal fibres of the spindle. The chromosomes assume the shape of a V with equal arms if it is metacentric, or with unequal arms if it is submetacentric. During anaphase, the microtubules of chromosomal

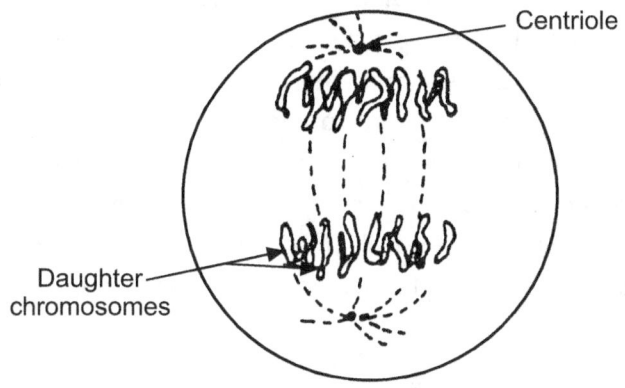

Fig. 9.6 : Early Telophase

spindle shorten one-third to one-fifth of the original length. Simultaneously, the microtubules of the continuous fibres increase in length. Some of these stretched spindle fibres constitute the interzonal fibres.

(4) Telophase : The end of the polar migration of daughter chromosomes marks beginning of telophase (Gr. *Telo* = end). The chromosomes start to fold and become less and less condensed, thus telophase is the reverse prophase. The spindle fibres disappear. The chromosomes gather into masses of chromatin that become surrounded by discontinuous segments of nuclear envelope made by the endoplasmic reticulum. Such segments fuse to make two complete nuclear envelopes of daughter nuclei.

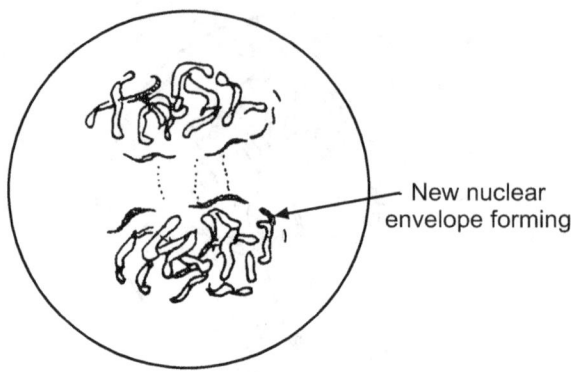

Fig. 9.7 : Middle Telophase

The nucleoli reappear at constrictions called the nucleolar organisers, in one pair of chromosomes. Each daughter cell gets the same complement of nuclei at the same sites as the parent cell.

Cytokinesis : Alongwith the unfolding of the chromosomes and formation of nuclear envelope, cytokinesis occurs. It is the process in which cell divides into two daughter cells and it differs in plant and animal cells. Cytokinesis in animal cells proceeds by the process of furrowing at the equatorial region. The furrow is accentuated and deepened until the cell divides. The two cells may be equal in size or quite unequal. In plant cells, there is formation of cell plate between two groups of chromosomes. The cell plate grows from middle towards the periphery and finally joins the cell-wall. This plate forms the membrane, separating the two cells. During cytokinesis, the cytoplasmic components are distributed including the mitochondria and golgi complex.

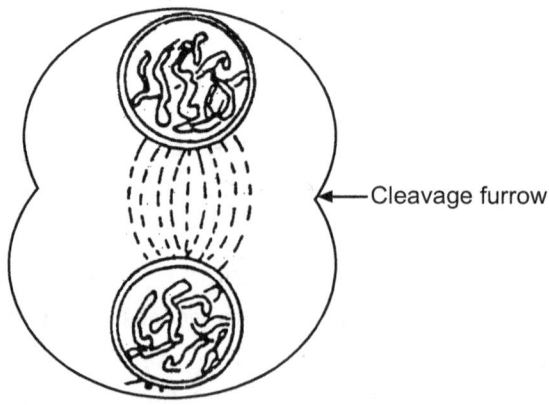

Fig. 9.8 : Late Telophase

Significance of Mitosis :

1. **Equal distribution of chromosomes :** In the process of mitosis, the chromosomes are equally distributed in two daughter cells. Thus, constant number of chromosomes in all the cells of the body is maintained due to mitosis.

2. **Surface volume ratio :** Mitosis also maintains surface volume ratio of the cell. As the cell increases in size, the available surface area in relation to increased volume, becomes less. Due to mitosis (or cell division) the cell becomes smaller in size and surface volume ratio is restored.

3. **Nucleoplasmic index :** A cell cannot grow in size to a large extent without disturbing the ratio between the nucleus and cytoplasm. After a particular size has been reached, the cell divides to maintain the nucleoplasmic index. Thus, growth takes place by an increase in the number of cells, rather than by increase in the size of the cells.

4. **Repair :** Repair of the body takes place by addition of cells by mitosis. There is constant replacement of epidermal cell, gut cell as well as red blood cells.

9.2 MEIOSIS

Meiosis is a special type of cell division found in organisms which reproduce by sexual reproduction. It occurs in the cells of gonads of animals and plants. The male and female gametes in sexually reproducing organisms fuse together and form the zygote. If the gametes had the same number of chromosomes as the somatic cells, then the zygote would have twice the diploid number of chromosomes. This number would go on doubling with each generation. But this never happens, as the chromosome number remains constant from generation to generation.

Meiosis is (Gr. meioum - to diminish) the mechanism that prevents chromosome from doubling. By series of two meiotic divisions, the number of chromosomes is reduced to half which counteracts the effect of fertilization. Thus, fertilization and meiosis are compensating events.

Meiosis essentially consists of two cell divisions which follow each other rapidly, while the chromosomes divide only once. The two divisions are known as the *first meiotic division* and *second meiotic division.*

9.2.1 Types of Meiosis

There are the following three types of meiosis :

1. **Zygotic or initial meiosis :** In this type, fertilization is immediately followed by meiosis, forming cell with haploid number of chromosomes. The zygote is the only **diploid** stage in the life-cycle and it occurs in lower plants.

2. **Gametic or terminal meiosis :** It occurs in humans, all animals, and few lower plants, just before the formation of gametes.

3. **Sporic or intermediate meiosis :** It occurs in higher plants and not in animals. It takes place between fertilization and the formation of gamete. In the diploid sporophyte meiosis takes place and forms megaspores and microspores. They undergo repeated mitosis and form gametophytes and certain cells differentiate to form gametes. Cells undergoing meiosis are often called *meiocytes.*

Following are the different stages of meiosis.

First meiotic division :

Prophase I $\begin{cases} \text{Preleptotene} \\ \text{Leptotene} \\ \text{Zygotene} \\ \text{Pachytene} \\ \text{Diplotene} \\ \text{Diakinesis} \end{cases}$

Pro-metaphase I

Metaphase I

Anaphase I

Telophase I

Second meiotic division :

Interphase or interkinesis

Prophase II

Metaphase II

Anaphase II

Telophase II

9.3 FIRST MEIOTIC DIVISION

(1) Interphase

The interphase preceding meiosis is important during this phase. DNA replication takes place, and it is confined to synthetic (S) phase of interphase.

(2) Prophase I

It is the first stage of meiosis and differs from prophase of mitosis. During this phase, nucleus starts increasing in volume due to hydration. It comprises mainly six substages, i.e. preleptotene, leptotene, zygotene, pachytene, diplotene and diakinesis.

(i) Preleptotene : It is the early prophase of meiosis. During preleptotene, the chromosomes are very thin and difficult to observe but only sex chromosomes may be seen.

(ii) Leptotene (Thin or slender thread) or Leptonema : During this period, the nucleus increases in size and the chromosomes become more distinct. Leptotene chromosomes look single rather than double. They appear as slender (thin) threads with bead-like thickenings called *chromomeres*. Because these beads are characteristic in size, number and position for a particular chromosome, they may be used as landmarks to identify a specific chromosome of an organism. Frequently, leptotene chromosomes have a definite polarization and form loops whose ends are attached to the nuclear envelope at points near the centrioles contained within an aster. This peculiar arrangement is often called the 'bouquet'. During leptotene phase, cytoplasm contains many polyribosomes, nucleolus increases and RNA and protein synthesis also increases.

(iii) Zygotene (mating thread) or Zygonema : During this stage, the chromosomes become shorter and thicker. The pairing or synapsis of homologous chromosomes begins. The homologous chromosomes undergo lengthwise pairing in which one chromosome has paternal origin (from male parent) called paternal chromosome, and other has maternal origin (from female parent) called maternal chromosome. This is the *bivalent stage*. Each pair of homologous chromosomes consists of four chromatids and this is sometimes referred to as *tetrad*. The pairing may begin at the centromere and proceed towards the end called *procentric pairing*. If it begins at the ends and proceeds towards the centromere, it is called *proterminal pairing*. Pairing is highly specific and involves the formation of a special structure that can be observed under the electron microscope and called *synaptonemal complex*. It lies between two homologous chromosomes as they do not fuse completely. This complex is composed of two lateral components or arms and a central or medial element. Each lateral component is shared by the two sister chromatids of homologue.

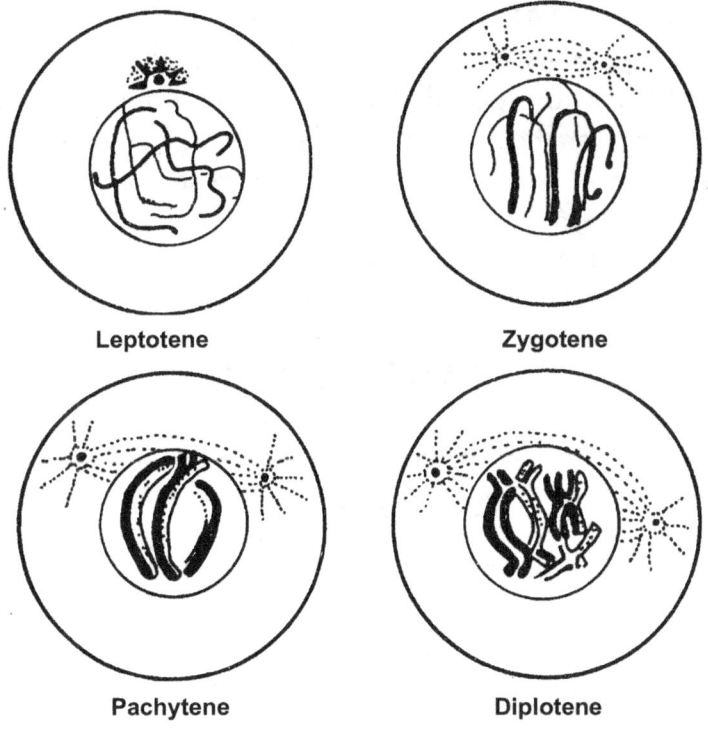

Leptotene   Zygotene

Pachytene   Diplotene

Fig. 9.9 : Meiotic Division Stages of Prophase I

Morphology of the synaptonemal complex is very similar in plant and animal cells. In cross-section, it appears flattened ribon-like structure. The lateral arms are formed of electron dense coarse granules or fibres. These arms are joined to the adjacent chromosomes by fine fibrils.

The synaptonemal complex is the structural basis for pairing and synapsis of meiotic chromosomes. The function of this complex is to stabilize the pairing between the homologues and to facilitate recombination.

(iv) Pachytene (Thick thread) or Pachynema : During this, the pairing of chromosomes is completed and it is a longer substage of prophase I. The chromosomes contract longitudinally so that threads become shorter and thicker. The chromosomes are associated in *bivalent* or *tetrads* composed of two homologous chromosomes in close longitudinal union and four chromatids. Each chromatid has its own centromere or kinetochore. Thus in a tetrad, first there are four centromeres, two homologous and two sister centromeres. During the first meiotic division, the centromeres of the two homologous chromatids behave as functional unit. The chromatid is the unit of crossing over. During pachytene, two chromatids belonging to different homologous chromosomes, undergo one or more transverse breaks at the same level. The breaks never occur between two sister chromatids. The break is followed by interchange and fusion of broken ends between two homologous chromosomes. This is called *crossing over*. Thus each bivalent consists of two chromatids which are unbroken and two chromatids whose broken ends have been interchanged.

(v) Diplotene or diplonema : During this stage, the intimately paired chromosomes repel each other and begin to separate. But this separation is not complete, because the homologous chromosomes are held together at one or more points where breaks and fusion have occurred. These points are called *chiasmata*. Chiasmata are generally regarded as the sites where the phenomenon of crossing over or recombination takes place. With few exceptions, chiasmata are found in all plants and animals.

Fig. 9.10 (a) : Chiasmata Formation

At least one chiasma is formed for each bivalent. Their number is variable, some chromosomes show one chiasma while others show several. During diplotene, the four chromatids of the thread become visible and the synaptonemal complex disappears. A chiasma formed at the ends of chromosomes is called *a terminal chiasma* and if formed along the lengths of chromosomes, it is called *interstitial chiasma.*

At the end of diplotene, the chiasma begins to move along the length of the chromosome from the centromere. This displacement is called *terminalization.* The terminal chiasma slips off the ends of the chromosomes and its position is taken up by an interstitial chiasma. The degree of terminalisation is expressed by the terminalisation coefficient (T).

$$T = \frac{\text{Number of terminal chiasma}}{\text{Total number of bivalents (or nuclei)}}$$

The frequency of chiasma (F_9) is the average number of chiasma in a bivalent or in bivalents of a nucleus.

$$F_9 = \frac{\text{Number of terminal chiasma}}{\text{Total number of bivalents (or nuclei)}}$$

The rotation is well marked in bivalent having one chiasma. The arms of the bivalent rotate through 180° and form a cross. If there are two chiasma, a bivalent loop is formed. With more than two chiasma, a series of loops are formed. Rotation is brought about by same forces of repulsion which bring about terminalization.

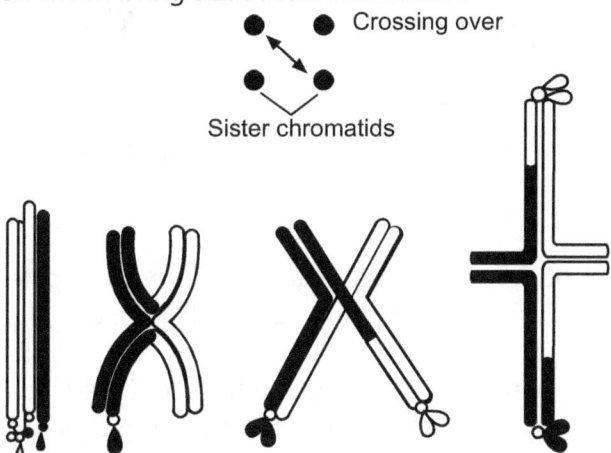

Fig. 9.10 (b) : Crossing-over, Chiasma Formation, Terminalization and Rotation

(vi) Diakinesis : In this phase, the chromosomes again contract. The tetrads (bivalents) are more evenly distributed in the nucleus and nucleolus disappears. During this period, number of chiasmata diminishes. By the end of diakinesis, the homologues are held together only at their ends.

(3) Pro-metaphase I

In this phase, condensation of the chromosomes reaches its maximum. The nuclear membrane breaks down and disappears. Spindle formation begins.

(4) Metaphase I

In this phase, the chromosomes become attached at the equator. The spindle is formed and the spindle fibres become attached to the centromeres of two homologous chromosomes. The two centromeres of each bivalent lie on opposite sides of equatorial plate. Metaphase I of meiosis differs from those of mitosis as there are bivalents, and each bivalent consists of two centromeres and they are being pulled towards the poles.

(5) Anaphase I

In anaphase I, the sister chromatids of each homologue, united by centromere move towards the poles of the cells. The short chromosomes separate rapidly, while the separation of long chromosomes is delayed due to interstitial chiasmata. By recombination, segments are transposed between two of the chromatids of each homologue. In each homologue chromosome, one chromatid is unchanged, while the other has undergone mixing of maternal and paternal sections. There is no division of centromeres as in anaphase of mitosis.

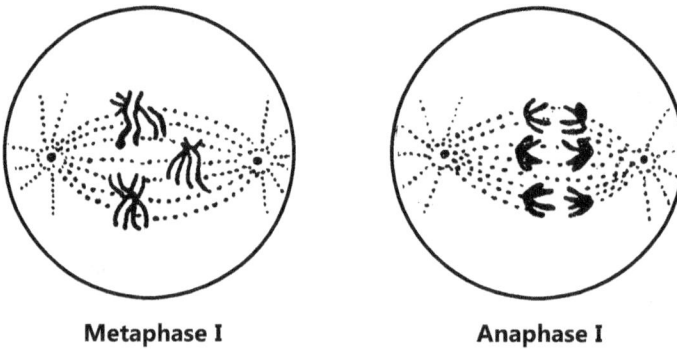

Metaphase I   Anaphase I

Fig. 9.11

(6) Telophase I

It begins when the chromosomes reach at their respective poles. Chromosomes may remain in a condensed state for sometime. Later they undergo, despolaralisation and become elongated. Nuclear membrane is reformed and spindle fibres do not disappear completely. By cytokinesis in animal cells, two daughter cells are formed. In most plant cells, daughter cells are formed by forming cells plate between two groups of chromosomes. In other plant cells, cytokinesis takes places after completion of both the meiotic divisions.

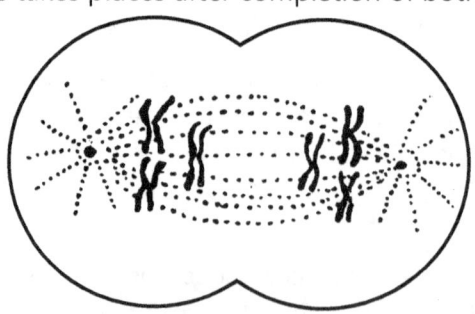

Fig. 9.12 : Telophase I

9.4 SECOND MEIOTIC DIVISION

(1) Interphase II or Interkinesis

The second meiotic division is similar to mitosis, however, there is no DNA duplication. After telophase I, two haploid daughter nuclei or cells sometimes undergo typical resting stage as in mitosis. This intervening stage between telophase I and beginning of prophase II is called *interphase II* or *interkinesis*. This differs from interphase I and interphase of mitosis as there is no DNA duplication.

Fig. 9.13 : Interkinesis or Interphase II

(2) Prophase II

This stage is of shorter duration and much simpler than prophase I. Chromosomes undergo shortening and thickening. The sister chromatids have already been separated. The two chromatids of each chromosome remain separate except at the centromere. Spindle formation takes place in prophase II and in mitosis nuclear membrane disappears.

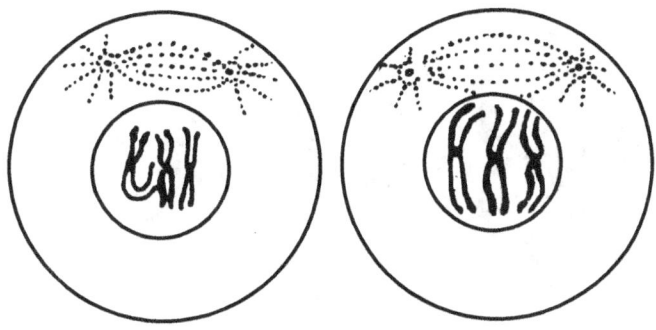

Fig. 9.14 : Prophase II

(3) Metaphase II

At this stage, chromosomes become arranged on the equatorial plane. The centromere of each chromosome splits longitudinally forming two centromeres. At the end of metaphase II, centromeres are connected to the spindle fibres from respective poles.

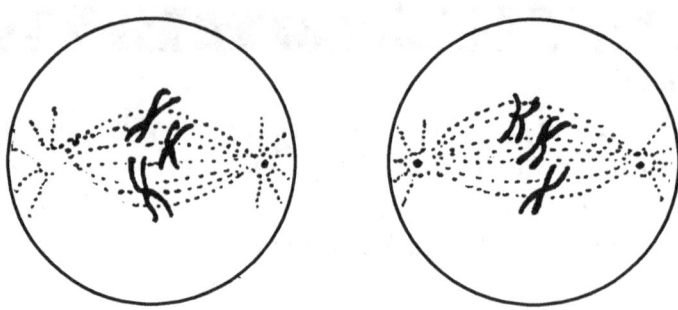

Fig. 9.15 : Metaphase II

(4) Anaphase II

It begins with the movement of chromatids to the opposite poles. They are pulled by contraction of spindle fibres.

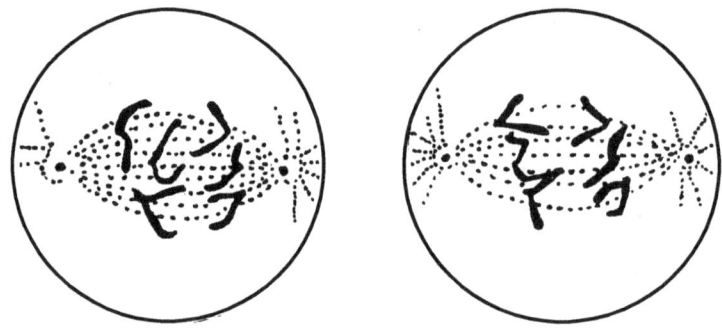

Fig. 9.16 : Anaphase II

(5) Telophase

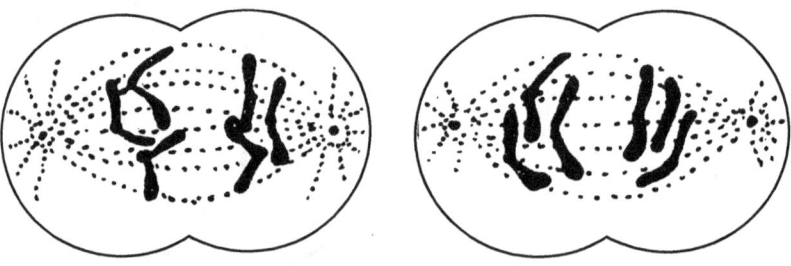

Fig. 9.17 : Telophase II

The movement of chromatids to opposite poles ultimately results in the formation of nucleus at each poles as in mitosis. The nucleus, centriole and the chromosomes return to the interphasic condition. From two haploid nuclei at the end of meiosis I, four haploid nuclei are formed after the completion of meiosis II. Thus, meiosis II is an equational division.

Cytokinesis

Cell walls are formed between the daughter nuclei after the completion of telophase I. In some species, cell walls develop simultaneously at the end of the second division, while in other species, a cell wall is formed at the end of meiosis I and then successively at the end of meiosis II. In both the cases, four cells with haploid number of chromosomes in their nuclei are formed.

Significance of Meiosis

Meiosis is a very important event in the life-cycle of sexually reproducing organisms. It is opposite of fertilization. In fertilization, the chromosome number is restored back to the original one, whereas meiosis reduces the chromosome number to half. The chromosomes in a species remain constant because of meiosis. For example, in human being, the somatic cells contain 46 chromosomes. If there will be no meiosis during gamete formation, the resultant gametes will carry 46 chromosomes. When the male and female gametes will fuse, the zygote will possess 92 chromosomes. In the next generation, the chromosome number will be doubled to 184. But such situation does not happen due to meiosis; and hence each gamete possesses haploid number chromosomes.

Fig. 9.18 : Daughter Cells

Secondly, there is reshuffling of genetic material during crossing over. This gives an opportunity for the exchange of genes between homologous chromosomes.

The separation of chromosomes at anaphase is at random, so the two nuclei formed at the end of meiosis I, are neither purely maternal nor paternal but random combination of both.

Random separation of chromosomes and crossing-over are responsible for the variations found in sexually reproducing organisms. Variations provide raw material for evolution.

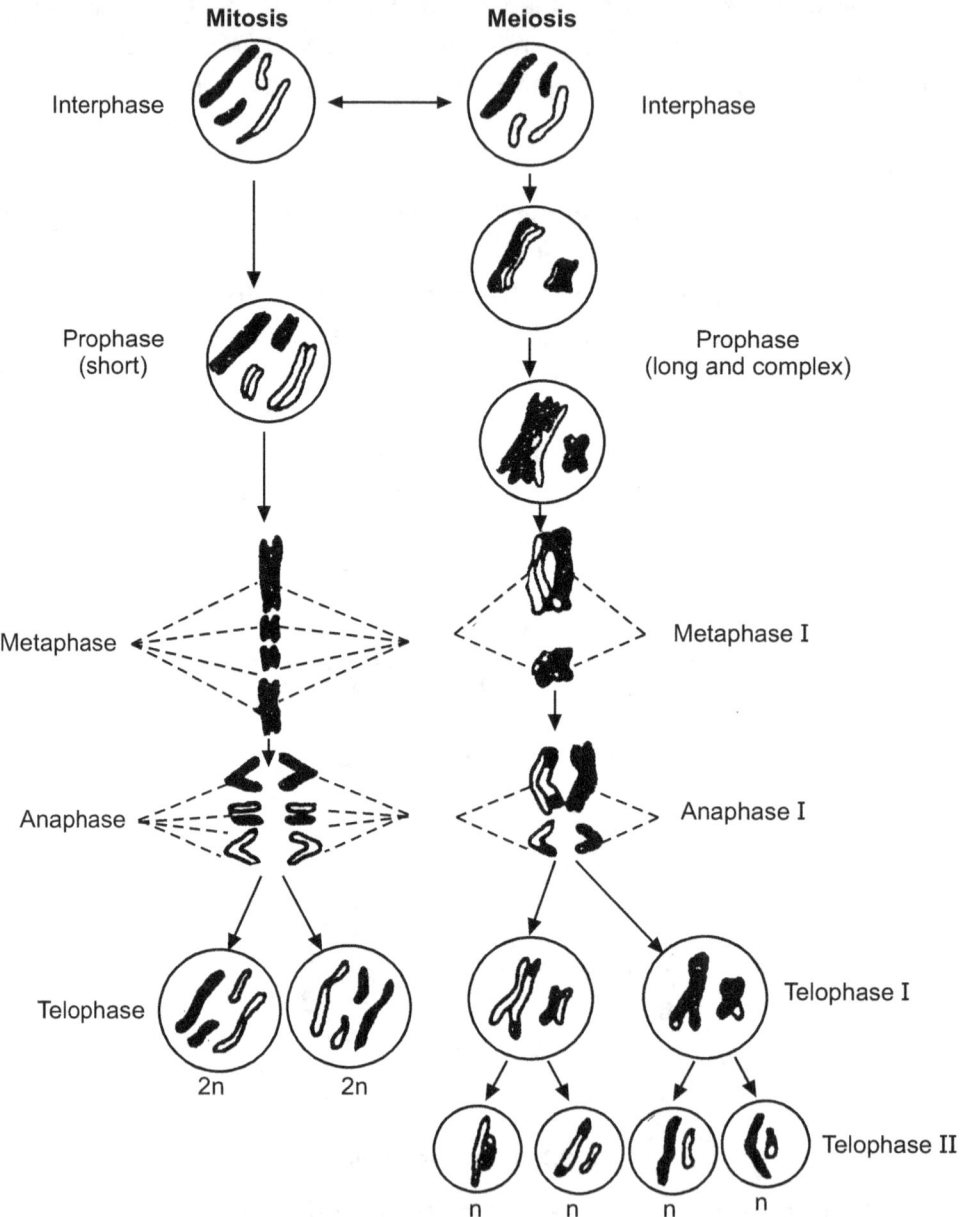

Fig. 9.19 : Comparative Diagram of Mitosis and Meiosis in Idealized Cells having Four Chromosomes (2n)

Comparison of Mitosis and Meiosis

	Mitosis	Meiosis
1.	The cell shows division only once.	The cell shows two cell divisions, the first and the second meiotic divisions.
2.	It occurs only in somatic cells.	Meiosis occurs in the germ cells only.
3.	It occurs in both sexually and asexually reproducing organisms.	It occurs only in sexually reproducing organisms.
4.	In mitosis DNA synthesis occurs in the S phase.	In meiosis there is premeiotic DNA synthesis which is much longer than that in mitosis.
5.	In mitosis every chromosome behaves independently.	In meiosis the homologous chromosomes become mechanically repeated during the first meiotic division.
6.	Mitosis is brief process of 1 or 2 hours.	Meiosis is long process. It lists few days to a several years.
7.	In mitosis, the genetic material remains constant.	In meiosis, genetic variability is one of the main consequences.
8.	In mitosis DNA replication occurs during interphase I.	DNA replication occurs during interphase I but not interphase II.
	Prophase	
9.	The prophase is of short duration usually of few hours.	The duration of prophase is long and takes several days or years.
10.	Prophase is very simple.	Prophase is complicated and divided into many substages such as leptotene and diakinesis.
11.	Chromosomes are double structures and consist of two chromatids united by centromere.	The two homologous chromosomes form bivalents or tetrads having four chromatids and two centromeres.
12.	There is no exchange of chromosomes during prophase.	There is exchange of segments of chromatids of homologous.
13.	The arms of the chromatids are close to one another.	The arms of chromatids are separated widely in prophase II.

Contd.

	Mitosis	Meiosis
	Anaphase	
14.	The centromeres lie towards the equator and arms directed towards the poles.	In metaphase I, the centromeres are lined up in two planes which are parallel to each other and their arms are directed towards equator.
15.	Metaphasic plate consists of chromosome pairs.	Metaphasic plate is made of paired chromosome pairs.
16.	The centromeres divide during anaphase.	No centromere division during anaphase II.
17.	There is also separation of chromosomes.	Short chromosomes separate rapidly but long chromosomes show delayed separation.
	Telophase	
18.	In telophase, spindle fibres disappear completely.	Spindle fibres do not disappear in telophase I.
19.	Nucleoli reappear at telophase.	Nucleoli do not reappear during telophase I.
20.	Cytokinesis always takes place after each division.	Cytokinesis is not necessary to occur in telophase I, but it normally extends to the second meiotic division.

Points to Remember

- The cell cycle is an ordered set of events, culminating in cell growth and division into two daughter cells.
- The cell cycle involves two major phases-growth phase or non-dividing phase or interphase and mitotic phase (karyokinesis) or Division phase.
- The G_1 phase occupies about 30 – 50% time of the complete cell cycle.
- The S-phase is the synthetic phase of interphase which involves replication of DNA and synthesis of histone proteins which are associated with DNA.
- It occupies about 35 – 45% time of the cell cycle.
- G_2 phase is the second gap or growth phase of the interphase which involves synthesis of ribosomal RNA, messenger RNA and nucleolar RNA.

- Mitosis is the multiplication of the somatic cells into daughter cells of equal size both containing the same number of chromosomes as the parent cell.
- During prophase, the nucleus enlarges and the chromosomes start to condense.
- The chromatids become shorter and thicker; chromosomes are evenly distributed in the nuclear cavity.
- At the end of prophase, the nuclear envelope is rapidly fragmented and disappears releasing nuclear material into the cytoplasm.
- During metaphase, the chromosomes are arranged radially at the equator to form the equatorial plate.
- During anaphase, the chromosomes arranged on equatorial plate divide and the two chromatids of each pair separate.
- During telophase, the chromosomes become less and less condensed and the spindle fibres disappear.
- Cytokinesis is the division of the cytoplasm of a cell following the division of the nucleus.

Exercise

1. Write an essay on cell cycle.
2. Describe somatic cell division or mitosis in an animal cell with suitable diagrams.
3. Give neat and labelled diagrams to explain mitosis.
4. Give a detailed account of the meiotic cell division and explain its significance.
5. Describe process of meiosis and compare it with mitotic cell division.
6. Describe significance of prophase-I of meiosis.
7. Differentiate between diplotene and pachytene.
8. Describe significance of mitosis and meiosis.
9. Explain the term cell cycle. Explain the different phases of the cell cycle.
10. Differentiate between mitosis and meiosis.
11. Write short notes:
    a. Significance of meiosis
    b. Cell cycle
    c. Cytokinesis
    d. Zygotene
    e. Pachytene
    f. Diplotene

   g.   Significance of mitosis

   h.   Anaphase

   i.   Interphase

   j.   Metaphase

   k. G_0 phase

12. Define the terms: cell cycle and mitosis. Name the stages of cell cycle.

13. What is Mitosis? Describe the different stages of mitosis.

14. Define mitosis and add a note on cell cycle.

15. What is meiosis? Add note on its significance.

16. Mention the similarities and differences between mitosis and meiosis.

17. How is meiosis necessary to sexual reproduction? What are the basic differences between mitosis and meiosis?

18. Describe the first meiotic division in brief.

19. Describe the second meiotic division and give its significance.

20. What is meiosis? Describe in detail the process of meiosis.

Chapter 10

CELL ADHESION

- CONTENTS -

10.1 CELL TO CELL CONTACT

The ability of the cells to recognise and adhere to one another has been studied in many organisms and cell types. From these studies it was observed that the cell surface molecules that are involved and the way in which they interact play an important role in cell adhesion. Just as integrins serve as transmembrane receptor that bind cells to the extracellular matrix, adhesion receptors serve to bind cells to one another. We now know that such adhesion receptors fall into a relatively small number of classes. They include immunoglobulin super family proteins, e.g. catherins, selectins and in a few cases, integrins.

In each case, the adhesion receptors on the surface of one cell binds to the appropriate ligand on the surface of a neighbouring cell. In some cases such as many catherins and immunoglobulin super-family members known as CAMs, cells interact with identical molecules on the surface of the cell to which they adhere. Such interactions are said to be homophilic interactions (Greek; homo = like and philia = friendship) in other cases, such as selections, a cell adhesion receptor on one cell interacts with a different molecule on the surface of the cell to which it attaches such interactions are called heterophilic interactions (Greek hetero-different). As with the intergrins, many transmembrane adhesion receptors attach to the cytoskeleton via linker proteins, which differ depending on the class of molecule and its location within the cell.

10.1.1 Lecithins

A role for carbohydrate groups in cell adhesion is also suggested by the fact that many animal and plant cells secrete carbohydrate binding proteins called lecithins, which promote cell-cell adhesion by binding to a specific sugar or sequence of sugars exposed at the outer cell surface. Because a lecithin molecule usually has more than one carbohydrate binding site, it can bind to carbohydrate groups on two different cells, thereby linking the cells together.

10.1.2 Cell Adhesion Molecules (CAMs)

These are the membrane glycoprotein from nerve tissue called neural cell adhesion molecule (N-CAM). Cell adhesion is mediated by the binding of N-CAMs located one cell to N-CAMs located on another cells. CAMs are members of the immunoglobulin super family (IgSF) and IgSF members participate in wide range of adhesion events, including interactions of lymphocytes with cells that mediate immune responses.

10.1.3 Cadherins

This is important group of glycoproteins found in the plasma membranes of most animal cells and they play a crucial role in cell-cell recognition and adhesion. They required calcium to function. If calcium is removed from cells they undergo dissociation.

10.2 CELL MOVEMENT

Cells also exhibit amoeboid motion which is characteristic of *Amoeba* and many free cells. In amoeboid motion, the cell changes shape actively, sending forth cytoplasmic projections called pseudopodia, into which the protoplasm flows. Although, this special form of locomotion can be observed easily in *Amoeba*, it also occurs in numerous other types of cells.

The leucocytes of the blood also show movement. They show first spheroidal shape than change their shape emit pseudopodia and move. In tissue cultures, cells move out actively forming the zone of migration. These changes also occur *in-vivo*. For example, in epithelial repair, the cells free themselves and slide along actively toward the depth of the wound. In an inflammatory process, leucocytes wander out of the blood vessels (dispedesis) by active amoeboid motion and progress towards the focus of infection.

Some *Amoeba* show only single pseudopodium called *monopodial* but the other amoeba are temporarily or permanently *polypodial*. The pseudopodia of *Amoeba* also show variation. The stout, cylindrical lobopodium or fine filamentous or branching *filopodium*. Processes may be anastomosing called reticulopodia which are found in *Foraminifera*.

Cell movements are best observed by time lapse photography and this study was done by **Lewis**. It was observed that after a few hours of culture, the fibroblasts acquired a polygonal shape with sheet-like extensions of the cytoplasm or *lamellipodia*. These are known as ruffled membranes, because they resemble the ruffles of a dress moving under the impulse of breeze. These ruffling lamellipodia constitute the main locomotive processes of amoeboid cells and are well studied by scanning electron microscopy. Culture cell sending lamellipodia to a glass surface and amoeboid motion is reversibly inhibtied by cytochalasin-B. These cells also give out thread like processes called filopodia and they perform the exploratory function i.e. the recognising the area in which the cell spreads. In developing neuron, *filopodia* are abundant and they serve a sensory function prior to the formation of more permanent contacts with other cells.

The ameboid cell does not adhere to the solid support by the entire bottom surface, but only by a small number of sites called *adhesion plaques*. During the movement of cell these sites of adhesion are continuously formed and broken.

Another experiment can be performed for study of amoeboid movement in which the cells are put on a glass coated with gold particles. Displacement can be easily followed, because the migrating cell phagocytizes the particles producing a particle free track. These tracts are called phagokinetic because they are the result of a combination of phagocytosis and locomotion. This method is useful for the study of the movement of a large number of cells. These tracks can be used to study the effect of substances that may stimulate or inhibit the movement of the migrating cells. One interesting observation is that after a cell division, the two daughter cells tend to follow symmetrical tracks that are mirror images of one another. For the movement of cell to a particular direction requires integrity of the whole cell.

This is revealed by the experiment in which fibroblasts are treated with cytochalasin-B. The cell forms tiny fragments of cytoplasm called mircoplast. These microplasts exhibit all known forms of amoeboid movement, but are unable to move in a certain direction. The rate of progression of different amoeba is different between 0.5 and 4.6 μm per second. The leucocyte show rate of progression is about 0.6 μm per second and this rate is modified by temperature and other environmental factors.

There are different substances which influence the motion by attracting or repelling the cells and this property is called *chemotaxis*. Which has great importance in defence mechanisms especially during inflammation.

Calcium is required for this type of locomotion. Mechanical injury, electrical shock, or ultraviolet radiation causes retraction of pseudopodia and actin-myosin interaction is the motive force for amoeboid movement. Some investigators give importance to posterior region of endoplasmic tube whereas some give more importance to the advancing end of amoeba.

Points to Remember

- The cell surface molecules that are involved and the way in which they interact play an important role in cell adhension.
- Lecithins, a carbohydrate binding proteins which promote cell-cell adhesion by binding to specific sugar or sequence by sugar exposed at outer cell surface.
- CAMs (Cell adhesion molecules) are members of immunoglobulin super family (IgSF) and IgSF members involve in adhesion events, including interactions of lymphocytes with cells that mediate immune responses.
- Cell also exibit amoeboid motion which is characteristic of Amoebae and many free cells.
- Cell moments are best observed by time lapse photography and this study was done by Lewis.

Exercise

1. What is cell adhesion ? Describe the mechanism of cell adhesion.
2. Define cell adhesion and add the note on chemicals involve in the process of cell adhesion.
3. Distinguish between homophilic interactions and Heterophilic interactions.
4. Describe the role of lecithin, CAMs and cadherins in cell adhesion.
5. What is cell movements ? Describe in brief the process of cell movements.
6. What is amoeboid movement ? Describe the experiments to explain amoeboid movement.
7. Write short notes on :
   (a) Amoeboid movement
   (b) Cell adhesion
   (c) Chemotaxis.

CELLULAR AGEING AND CELL DEATH

- CONTENTS -

The process of ageing is an inevitable biological event that can neither be stored nor stopped. The science that studies biological causes of senescence is called *gerontology*. Thus, ageing can be defined as a process occurring in all the members of a population after maturity, involving progressive decline in vital capacities of the organism, terminating in death. The process of ageing is progressive and not reversible under physiological condition.

Ageing in Cells : In the process of ageing, there is cessation of growth. There are three ageing processes have been under study at the cellular level.

(i) Possible decline in the final efficiency of non-dividing highly specialized cells, such as neurons and muscle cells.

(ii) Progressive stiffening with age of the structural protein collagen.

(iii) Limitation on cell division as revealed by the studies on fibroblasts, producing collagen and fibrin.

11.1 CONCEPTS OF AGEING THEORIES

There are several theories of ageing are being put forward because of our insight into the molecular mechanisms of ageing at the sub-cellular or intracellular level is increasing. But there is hardly any single theory that can explain the mechanism of ageing. Following are the some of the theories explained here.

Free Radical Theory of Ageing : According to **Harman**, ageing process is probably due to cumulative degradative changes brought about by free radical reactions. These reactions are ubiquitous in all living systems, which are deleterious and hasten biological degredation associated with ageing. During these reactions highly reactive intermediate products are formed called free radicals. These free radicals have free electrons and they have high chemical reactivity and the reactions are irreversible. For example: the reactions of oxygen with gasoline in an automobile engine, drying of linseed oil, paints, smog formation and development of rancidity in butter are some of the common free radical reactions.

In case of biological systems molecular oxygen is always present, which participates in free radical reactions involving organic compounds.

$$RH + O_2 \xrightarrow{\text{Cu}} R + HO_2$$

$$R + O_2 \longrightarrow RO_2$$

$$RO_2 + RH \longrightarrow R + ROOH$$

$$R + R \longrightarrow R : R$$

Free radical reactions are enhanced by catalysts such as copper, iron and managanese and inhibited by antioxidants such as vitamin E, 2 mercaptoethyl amine and butylated hydroxyltolune that are capable of removing intermediate free radicals.

(2) Somatic Mutation Theory : Each individual of a particular species has certain life span. It is because the genetically controlled programmes become progressively less effective until death. Therefore, an individual is more vulnerable to death. This is the result of age related damage in the genetic material of cell i.e. DNA. Changes in the base sequence of DNA alter the template and affect the regulatory and metabolic capabilities of the cell. Damage to the genetic material of cell or genome occurs due to radiation, replicating errors caused by mismatched nucleotides. These are nothing but mutations. The alterations which occur in the genome of somatic cells and not in the germ cell is called somatic mutation.

According to **Orgel**, the ability of the cell to produce enzymes depend on the correct specification of aminoacids in polypeptide chain and proper protein synthesis machinery. Error or disturbance in the information system makes existence of the cell critical. Based on this idea Orgel formulated the concept of error catastrophe which arise in somatic cells. In such cells, there is no selection by mitosis, as selection would ensure accurate transcription and translation. This results in the production of faulty enzymes or proteins and these incorrect amino acids are responsible to enhance the ageing process. Such non-functional proteins are accumulated in the cell with progressive ageing.

The hypothesis of **Orgel** was experimentally tested by *R. Holliday* and his co-workers in the larva of *Drosophila melanogaster* by incorporation of false amino acids. This resulted into appreciably reduced the life span of adult flies. In addition to this many other experiments also revealed that the biologically non-functional proteins increase in the cell with age. Experiments with ageing cell cultures of human lung fibroblasts of MRC- 5 strain have shown that non-functional enzyme molecules are produced that increase with ageing. Thus, this hypothesis confirmed that altered proteins are responsible for enhancing the ageing process.

Thus, in the ageing cell, there are changes in the information content takes place and mistakes in protein synthesis are incorporated. Some of the mechanisms are outlined below :

(1) The mistake in metabolic DNA give rise to defective DNA and it is not replaced or corrected in the ageing cell. These faulty molecules are accumulated in the cell and impair the metabolic functions.

(2) The information content of DNA can also be modified by chemical changes. It has been reported that the number of methyl groups in DNA decreases with age. This would involve structural changes in the regions which are rich in cytosine guanine.

(3) According to another existing hypothesis that the ageing is due to loss of non-repetitive DNA. In the encaryotic cells highly repetitive DNA sequences are found in the genome, which help in reinforcing the expression of genetic information.

Immunological Hypothesis of Ageing : According to this hypothesis, the changes in the genome of somatic cells modify cellular functions. The cells exhibit limit to the number of cell generations called *Hayflick limit*. Therefore, after 50-100 generations mitosis in the cell lines fails. In human fibroblast cell culture, malignant cell lines show no such limited growth. Thus, it has been reported that ageing is mediated by immunological interactions among populations of mobile cells within the body. It is possible in to two ways :

(1) With the appearance of altered antigens, immune responses against the changed cells become possible.

(2) Mutation within lymphocytes (immunocytes) can change qualities concerned with tolerance to self components normal to the body and on occasion give rise to clone with potential auto immune pathogenicity.

11.1.1 Intracelluar Mechanism of Ageing

Normal cells have a finite limit of division. The functional changes occur intracelluarly which produce age related changes. Orgel in 1963, put forward a hypothesis suggesting that cellular ageing results from impaired specificity of the translation step in protein synthesis.

(1) Change in Functioning of Nucleic acid : Normally, cell metabolism is continuously regulated by interactions of nucleic acids and their enzymes but after sometime there is failure in function of nucleic acids. This defective functioning is the result of quantitative changes in the nuclei acid content.

(2) Quantitative Changes : Loss of DNA or RNA per cell with increasing age may be able to explain the decline in the functional efficiency.

(3) Changed Information Content : During the life span of an individual accumulation of gene mutations in the somatic cells bring about the synthesis of faulty proteins.

(4) Changes in Protein Regulatory Mechanism : Loss of specificity of enzymes would lead to loss of information at the level of operon regulatory mechanism. The cellular ageing may be a result of failure or switch-over of regulatory processes. Changes in RNA, PODI in old age have been observed. Random errors affecting metabolism interfere with this programme. It is experimentally proved that there is functional impairment of intra nuclear regulatory processes.

11.1.2 Extracellular Changes in Ageing

There are also age related changes in the tissues outside the cell, particularly they are observed in the connective tissues. Synthesis of collagen declines rapidly at a relatively advanced stage. The elasticity of skin and blood vessels is due to elastic fibres which diminish in quantity with ageing. Arteriosclerosis is important disease of ageing. With increasing age the concentration of structural glycoproteins decreases and lipids derived from degradation of lipoproteins are deposited to make them less elastic. This is loss of control and co-ordination of genetic programme and hence cells either synthesize wrong molecules or simply stop synthesizing. The important factor is the mechanical stress produced by environment, lack of nutrition and physical exercise. Lack of exercise reduce the good functioning of tissues.

11.2 CELL DEATH

All metabolic activities of the body are carried out and regulated by the cells of the tissues. The cell tends to preserve its intracellular milieu within a relatively narrow range of physiological parameters. It maintains normal homeostasis. As the cell encounters physiologic stresses or pathologic stimuli, it undergo adaptation, achieving a new steady state and preserving viability. The principal adaptive responses are atrophy (decrease in size), hypertrophy (increase in size) hyperplasia and metaplasia alteration of cell structure. If the cell's adaptive capability is exceeded cell injury develops upto a point, cell injury is reversible however with severe or persistent stress, the cell suffers irreversible injury and ultimately dies.

These several factors which causes cell injury like hypoxia, physical agents like trauma, extremes of temperatures, radiation, electric shock, sudden changes in atmospheric pressure, chemicals and drugs, microbiological agents, genetic defects, immunological reactions and nutritional imbalance :

(1) Necrosis

(2) Apoptosis

(3) Necrobiosis

(1) Necrosis : Necrosis means the death of cells or groups of cells. It may occur suddenly, for example, when cells are exposed to heat or toxic chemicals.

Causes of Necrosis :

(a) **Marked Impairment of Blood Supply :** It is due to obstruction of an end artery which is a common and important cause of necrosis.

(b) **Toxins :** Certain bacteria, plants, animals such as snakes and scorpions, produce toxic organic compounds which are in very small quantities can cause cell damage amounting to necrocis.

(c) **Immunological Injury :** Cell injury results in various ways from immune reactions. This is feature of many infections.

(d) **Infection of Cells :** In certain infections particularly by viruses, kill cells in tissues.

(e) **Chemical Poisons :** Many chemicals in high concentration cause necrosis e.g. strong acids, strong alkalies, mercuric chloride, cyanide.

(f) **Physical Agents :** Heat, cold, mechanical trauma radiation are also responsible to necrosis.

(2) Apoptosis : Many normal cell types including blood cells undergo apoptosis. Apoptosis is nothing but programmed cell death. It is a relatively distinctive and important mode of cell death. It is responsible for the programmed cell death in several physiological and pathological processes including :

(a) The programmed destruction of cells during embryogenesis, as occurs in implantation, organogenesis and developmental involution.

(b) Hormone dependent physiological involution, such as the endometrium during menstrual cycle, or lactating breast after weaning or pathological atrophy, as in the prostate after castration.

(c) Cell deletion in proliferating populations such as intestinal cypt epithelium or cell in tumours.

(d) Deletion of autocreactive T cell in the thymus, cell death of cytokine starved lymphocytes or cell death induced by cytotoxic T cells.

(3) Necrobiosis : When necrosis preceded by gradual and potentially reversible damage in which case the term necrobiosis is occasionally used. Skin is affected by many of the granulomatous diseases. The skin is also exposed to injury, with lodgement of foreign material which stimulates granulomatous reaction. Necrobiosis *lipoidica* has been associated traditionally with diabetes but may also occur in non-diabetics.

The lesion appear most often in the legs as redish patches which slowly spread and have yellow centre. Scaring occurs and ulceration is occasionally seen. In this condition, a central area of collagen degeneration is surrounded by an infiltrate of mucrophages.

Difference between Apoptosis and Necrosis

	Apoptosis	Necrosis
1.	It is the programmed cell death.	It is the death of cells or groups of cells.
2.	It is distinctive and important mode of cell death.	It may occur suddenly or when cells are exposed to heat of toxic chemicals.
3.	It involves physiological and pathological processes like embryogenesis, implantation, organogenesis and developmental involution.	It occurs due to impairment of blood supply, or effect of toxins, immunological injury, infection of cells, chemical toxic substance or physical agents like heat, cold.

Points to Remember

- Ageing can defined as a process occurring in all the members of populations after maturity, involving progressive decline in vital capacities of the organisms terminating in death.

- Free radical theory and Somatic Mutation theory are theories of ageing. But hardly any single theory that can explain the mechanism of ageing.

- Normal cells have a finite limit of division. But in 1963, put forward a hypothesis suggesting that cellular ageing results from impaired specificity like change in functioning of nucleic acid, quantitative changes, changed information content changes in protein regularoty mechanism.

- Necrosis means the death of cells. It may occur suddenly, for example : Toxin, chemicals poisons, infection of cells.

- Apoptosis is nothing but programmed cell death and it is distinctive and important mode of cell death.

- Necrosis, it is death of cells or groups of cells, which occur suddenly or when cells are exposed to heat of toxic chemicals.

Exercise

1. What is cellular ageing ? Give an account of theories of ageing.
2. Describe intracellular mechanism of ageing.
3. Write short notes on :
   (a) Free radical theory of ageing
   (b) Somatic mutation theory
   (c) Immunological hypothesis of ageing
   (d) Intracellular mechanism of ageing
   (e) Extracellular mechanism of ageing
4. What is cell death? Describe different patterns of cell death.
5. Write short notes on :
   (a) Necrosis
   (b) Apoptosis
   (c) Necrobiosis
   (d) Cell death

❖ ❖ ❖

Chapter **12...**

CANCER CELL

- CONTENTS -

12.1 INTRODUCTION

In all multicellular organisms, cell division is normal phenomenon. Due to cell division, growth and repair takes place. Dead cells are replaced. Most of the cells undergo cell division except some cells like liver and brain which rarely divide in mature adult. Cell division is controlled process. Sometimes, however, cell division becomes very fast and uncontrolled leading to abnormal growth of cells causing disorder called *Cancer*. It should be noted that rapid growth means a high rate of cell division for a particular cell type. For example, the blood forming cells show very fast rate of cell division. Which is faster than the cancerous cells.

In cancer, the cells undergo rapid, abnormal and uncontrolled growth at the cost of remaining cells are called neoplastic cells. These cells form growth called neoplastic growth or tumours. These tumours are classified into two types : One type is called *benign* and another type is called *malignant*. In benign tumours, usually contain well-differentiated cells. Tumour cells are carried by blood stream or by lymphatic system or may directly penetrate other tissues where they may induce secondary tumours. Benign tumours can sometimes be fatal. For example, brain tumours can cause pressure on vital centres.

Types of Cancer : Cancer is not a single disease but a complex of many diseases. About 200 distinct types of cancers have been recognized. These are classified into four types.

(i) **Carcinomas :** These tumours are made up of mainly epithelial cells of ectodermal or endodermal origin. These include cervical, breast, skin and brain carcinomas. About 85% of cancers are carcinomas.

(ii) **Sarcomas :** These are the tumours made up of principally of connective tissue cells. Which are of mesodermal origin. These tumours are formed from connective tissue, cartilage, bone and muscle. They constitute about 2% of human cancers.

(iii) **Lymphomas :** This type of cancer show excessive production of lymphocytes by lymph nodes and spleen. This type constitutes about 5% of human cancers.

(iv) **Leukemias :** When neoplastic growth of leucocytes (W.B.C.) occurs due to excessive production of the cells, called *Leukemias*. They constitute about 4% of human cancers.

12.2 CHARACTERISTICS OF CANCER CELLS

Almost all types of differentiated cells can become cancerous. When cells loses its ability to control its rate of division and become a tumor cell. This process is called cell transformation. Generally, the cancer cell retains the structural and functional characteristics of the normal cell type from which it is derived. Thus, cancerous cells of thyroid gland continue to secrete thyroxin. Neo-plastic cells however, differ from their normal counterpart in several respect.

(1) Immortalization : Normal cell cultures do not survive indefinitely. For example, human cell cultures die after about 50 generations, chicken cell cultures have a much shorter life expectancy. On the other hand transformed cell cultures are immortal and can grow indefinitely.

(2) Loss of contact inhibition : In case of normal cells, a culture stop growing when their plasma membranes come into contact with one another. Thus, cells show growth inhibition and division. But in case of cancerous cells the cells usually do not stop dividing after forming monolayer. Division continues until several layers are formed and finally stage reaches that they kill themselves. Their cell membrane properties also change. They become less adhesive. These cells dissociates from neighbouring cells and infiltrate other organs and form secondary tumours. Cancerous cells lack proper recognition and communication.

(3) Invasiveness : Cancerous cells show ability to invade other tissues. This takes place due to change in properties of plasma membrane.

(4) Loss of anchorage dependence : The normal cells show attachment to the subtratum for growth. But in case of cancerous cells they grow without attachment with subtratum. Thus, these cells form malignant tumours.

(5) Lower serum requirement : For the growth of normal cells in tissue culture medium, a high concentration of serum is required but for cancerous cells very less serum is required in growth medium.

(6) Molecular changes in cell membrane : Normal and cancerous cells show differences in molecular changes in cell membrane components. The cell membrane consists of four important phospholipids. In case of cancer cells relative amount of glycolipids and enzymes are reduced. Molecular weight is also reduced.

(7) Changes in cytoskeleton : Normal cells contains microtubules, microfilaments which bring about co-ordinated cell movement. But in cancerous cells the normal architecture is changed and cytoskeleton is reduced.

(8) Increased sugar transport : Cancerous cells require more sugar for growth and multiplication. Hence, sugar transport also increases.

(9) Defective electrical communication : Normal cells show electrical communication among them but in cancer cells this connection is defective.

(10) Increased rate of glycolysis : Tumour cells shows depressed oxidative respiration (aerobic respiration) and increased glycolysis (anaerobic respiration).

(11) Aldolases : In most mammalian tissues, the enzyme aldolase exists in the form of isozymes A, B and C. Isozymes A and C predominate in embryonic tissues, while in adult differentiated tissues, the B isozyme is predominant. In some tumours, especially in poorly differentiated and rapidly growing cancers like hepatomas, isozyme B is replaced by isozyme A, the embryonic form.

(12) The cancer cells can grow in the suspension but normal cells cannot grow in it.

12.3 CAUSES OF CANCER

There are many agents including physical, chemical and biological agents have been found to include cancer in both experimental animals and humans. Agents which cause cancers are called *Carcinogens*. These external agents which are responsible for causing cancer are called *extrinsic causes.*

Physical agent like Radiation (solar ultraviolet ray, X-ray), chemical agent like carcinogens act by damaging DNA and inducing somatic mutations. These carcinogens are called initiating agents because the induction of mutations in key target genes is supposed to be the intial event leading to cancer development. There are different initiaing agents that cause human cancers include solar ultraviolet radiation, the major cause of skin cancer. The exposure of the thyroid gland to X-rays greatly increases the incidence of thyroid cancers. Varieties of chemical carcinogens including tobacco smoke containing benzopyrene, dimethyl nitrosamine and nickel compound and aflatoxin produced by some molds are the major identified cause of human cancer.

Other carcinogens induce the cancer development by stimulating cell proliferation rather than inducing mutations. Such compounds are called *tumour promoters.*

The people who use snuff suffers from nasal cancer. Chimney sweepers suffer from *Scrotum cancer* in their youth. After industrial revolution more and more incidences of cancer were reported among the workers who were continuously exposed to industrial chemicals. Repeated application of coal tar to rabbit skin causes tumour to develop, but the tumour disappear when application of the coal tar is stopped. It is also observed that when the skin is treated with terpentine, tumour again reappears. Normally, turpentine does not cause cancer itself. Therefore, the coal tar and turpentine are playing two different roles. Some carcinogens induce some normal cells to become irreversibly altered to a preneophatic state. This is known as initiation and the carcinogens are known as initiation agents. Here coal tar is a initiating agent. On the other hand, some carcinogens stimulate the preneoplastic cells to divide and form tumour. This is known as promotion and the carcinogens are termed as promoting agents. Here turpentine behaves as promoting agents.

Berenblum observed that painting the skin of mouse a single time with methyl cholanthren rarely causes the development of tumour. But subsequently, application of castor oil. Triggers the formation of multiple tumours on the skin which has been exposed previously to methyl cholanthren. Methyl cholanthren is acting as an initiator whereas castor oil acts as a promoter.

Table 12.1 : Chemical Carcinogens and Type of Cancer induced by Such Chemical

Sr. No.	Carcinogen	Types of Cancer induced
1.	Acrylonitrile	Colon, lung
2.	Asbestos	Lung
3.	Arsenic compounds	Skin, lung
4.	Benzene	Leukemia
5.	Carbon tetrachloride	Liver
6.	Lead	Kidney
7.	Nickel	Lung, nose
8.	Organochloride pesticides	Liver
9.	Polychlorinated biphenyls	Liver
10.	Soot and tars	Skin, lung, Bladder
11.	Vinyl chloride	Liver, lung, brain
12.	Wood and leather dust	Nasal sinuses
13.	Tobaco smoke	Lung, oval cavity, oesophagus, larynx, stomach, pancreas

Initiation is a quick, irreversible process that causes a permanent changes in a cell's DNA. The carcinogenic chemicals that act as initiating agent, are capable of binding to DNA.

Hence, they interfere with the normal function of DNA and induce somatic mutation and consequently bring about a stable, inheritable changes in the cell's properties.

There are two types of chemical carcinogens acting on DNA, one is direct acting and other is indirect acting. The direct acting carcinogens are highly electrophilic react with DNA and indirect carcinogens first metabolized before they can react with DNA.

Energy that travel through space is known as *Radiation*. Natural source of radiation to which humans are generally exposed are ultraviolet rays, cosmic rays and emission from radioactive elements. We are also exposed to another high energy radiation like X-ray. Medical, industrial and military activities generally create the high energy radiation.

(1) Sunlight : Sunlight has ability to cause skin cancer in people who are exposed to sunlight for long period. Sunlight contains ultraviolet rays which are also absorbed by normal skin pigmentation. Therefore, black skinned people usually have lower rates of skin cancer than fair (white) skinned individuals.

(2) X-rays : X-rays are high energy radiation. They can penetrate through the skin and reach internal organs. Thus, X-rays are hazardous and cancerous because they are able to induce gene mutation or DNA damage.

(3) Radioactive Elements : Many radioactive elements emit radiation. It also acts as carcinogen and causes cancer. Marie Curie co-discoverer of the radio active elements polonium and radium died due to leukemia. Another incidence occurred in New Jersey in 1920, a women working in watch factory who used fine tipped brush for painting the radium frequently wetted with their tongue. Minute quantities of radioactive substance was swallowed and they suffered from bone cancer. The most horrible example of radiation induced cancer occurred in Japan during second world war in which atomic bombs were exploded over Hiroshima and Nagasaki. People suffered from *leukemia, lymphomas* and cancers of thyroid, breast, uterus and gastrointestinal tracts.

(4) Viruses : There are many viruses which are capable of causing tumour in animals, human as well as plants. These viruses are called tumour viruses. Some tumour viruses have DNA genome and are known as DNA tumour viruses. Some tumour viruses have RNA genome and are known as *retorviruses*. In addition HIV is indirectly responsible for the cancer that develops in AIDS patients as a result of immunodeficiency. The *Herpes viruses* cause tumour in many animals such as frogs, chickens and monkeys.

12.3.1 Oncogenes

Oncogene is a type of specific viral gene that is capable of inducing cancer or cell transformation either in the body of host or in the tissue in culture.

After the discovery of *src* oncogene in RSV (Rous Sarcoma Virus), more than 40 different highly oncogenic retroviruses have been isolated from a variety of animals like mice, rat, cat, chickens, turkeys, monkeys etc. All the viruses contain atleast one oncogen like RSV. These oncognes are not needed for viral replication but is responsible for cell transformation. In some cases different viruses contain the same oncogenes. Many of these genes encodes protein which in turn acts as the key components of signaling pathways that induces cell transformation.

The normal counter part of oncogens are found in our normal cells.

Types of oncogens :

(1) Genes that code for growth factors.

(2) Genes that code for growth factor receptors.

(3) Genes that control cell cycle etc.

12.3.2 Tumour Suppressor Genes and their Role

Presence of an oncogene can stimulate uncontrolled cell growth and division, thereby fostering the development of malignancy. Cancer can also be included by the loss of tumour suppressor genes that normally inhibit cell proliferation. The term tumour suppressor gene implies that normal function of gene of this type is to restrain cell growth and division. In other words, tumour suppressor genes act as breakes on the process of cell, proliferation and inhibits tumour development. In many tumours, these genes are lost or inactivated, thereby removing negative regulators of cell proliferation and contributing to the abnormal proliferation of tumour cells. Normally, the function of tumour suppressor gene is just opposite to onocogene. The activity of tumour suppressor gene came from somatic cell function experiment done by Henry Harris *et.al.* in 1969. The fusion of tumour cells with normal cell yields hybrids that contain chromosomes from both parent. Such hybrids are usually non-tumourigenic. Supresssion of tumourigenicity by cell fusion indicates that genes derived from the normal cell definitely suppress the tumour development.

The first suppressor gene to be identified is involvement in hereditary retinoblastoma (RBI), a type of eye cancer that develops in young childhood who have a family history of the disease. Several other tumour suppressor genes have been identified. The second suppressor gene is P^{53} which is frequently inactivated in a wide variety of human cancer including leukemias, lymphomas, sarcomas, brain tumour and carcinomas of many tissues including breast, colon and lung. Like P^{53}, the INK_4 is a tumour suppressor gene that prevents lung cancer. Similarly, two other tumour suppressor genes such as APC and DCC prevent colon cancer. When these genes are detected or mutated, then such cancers develop.

12.3.3 Theories/Hypotheses about Cancer

There are several hypotheses to explain why a cell becomes cancerous. The main three hypotheses considered are somatic mutation hypothesis, the viral genes hypothesis and defective immunity hypothesis.

(1) The Somatic Mutation Hypothesis : As per this hypothesis the cancer is the result of somatic mutation without viral infection occurring in a cell. Such mutation is responsible for alteration of control mechanism of cell leading to uncontrolled cell division. In the mutations, the repressed genes are activated. This occurs because of mutations in the repressed genes themselves and mutations that block the production of repressor proteins, thus unblocking inactive genes and making them active.

The cancerous cells possess abnormal chromosomal components. The cells of tumour possess different number of chromosomes. In patients with chronic myeloid leukemia a large part of the long arm of chromosome number 22 is lost. Such chromosomes are called Philadelphia chromosomes. In such patients chromosomes of bone marrow shows abnormalities.

The patients suffering from retinoblastoma the middle segment of chromosome 13 is missing.

There are two types of chromosomes in the cells called effectors (E) chromosomes which cause malignancy and suppressor (S) chromosomes which suppress malignancy. Whether a cell is malignant or not depends upon a balance in the number of E and S chromosomes.

(2) The Vital Gene Hypothesis : These are number of viruses which are responsible for member of specific cancers in animals. The viruses causing malignant tumours have been isolated from different animals like mice, fish, frogs, rats, squirrels, dog, deer and horses. The polyoma virus has been isolated from mice and the **simian virus 40** (SV_{40}) from monkeys. Tumour producing viruses are called oncoviruses. But however, there is no clear cut evidence of malignant tumours caused in humans by viruses. Even no infective viruses have been isolated from cell cultures such as **HeLa cells**. This does not mean, that viruses are not causing cancer in man. There are several difficulties in trying to determine a virus cancer relationship in humans. There are viruses like **Epstein-Barr virus** (EB virus) with Burkitt's lymphoma, at tumour occurring in certain regions of Africa. The virus has been isolated from tumour cells of almost all patients. These are also found in nasopharyngeal carcinoma found in certain Chinese populations. **Herpes simplex** type virus has often been found associated with cervical cancer. Virus like RNA-DNA particles have been isolated from the patients of breast cancer and acute leukemia. The wart virus is known to cause growths, however, warts are benign and not malignant growths.

These observations do not establish a virus cancer relationship but virus like particles have been observed in human tumour cells and such particles have also been seen in normal cells.

(3) The Defective Immunity Hypothesis : The rate of spontaneous mutations is higher than the frequency of tumours. It can be concluded that, there must be some mechanism for suppressing mutations resulting in cancer or the newly formed cancer cells must be destroyed in same way. In newly formed cancer cells are destroyed by the immunological responses of the cell. This is called immunological surveillance. Cancerous cells contain antigens not found in ordinary cells.

According to the defective immunity hypothesis the defense mechanism fails under certain conditions and tumours are formed. This is because the number of immune lymphocytes may not be large enough to block tumour development. The cause of production of insufficient number of lymphocytes is not known. It may be mutation in the lymph cells, poor nutrition, emotional stress or other factors.

Points to Remember

- In multicellular organisms cell division is normal phenomenon, but sometimes division become very fast and uncontrolled leading to abnormal growth of cells called cancers.
- Cancers tumours are classified into two types : Benign and Malignant tumours.
- Cancer cell classified into four types : Carcinomas, Sarcomas, lymphomas and leukemias.
- There are many agents including physical, chemicals and biological agents which is responsible for causing cancers.
- Oncogene is a type of specific viral gene that is capable of including cancer or cells transformation either in the body of host or tissue in culture.

Exercise

1. What is Cancer ? Describe different types of cancers.
2. Define the term cancer and describe different characterisitcs of Cancer cell.
3. What are the causes of Cancer ? Describe in brief different agents responsible for cancer.
4. What is oncogene ?
5. What is Tumour Supressor gene ? Give its role.
6. Give an account of theories or hypothesis of cancer.
7. Write a short notes on :
   (a) Cancer
   (b) Characteristics of cancer cell
   (c) Physical agents of cancer
   (d) Chemical agents of cancer
   (e) Oncogenes
   (f) Tumour suppressor genes
   (g) Types of cancer
   (h) Tumour causing viruses.

www.ingramcontent.com/pod-product-compliance
Lightning Source LLC
Chambersburg PA
CBHW080329040726

47501CB00020B/2423